# MURDER AT WHISPERING KEY

## A Whispering Key Mystery

By

Sharon Colvin & Terri Borkgren

Cricket Cottage Publishing

For information about group sales and permission, contact Cricket Cottage Publishing, LLC, 1889 South Kirkman Road, Suite 614, Orlando, Florida 32811 or call 407-255-7785.

Cover art by Mackeigan Wuest



ISBN: 978-0615865430
ISBN-10: 0615865437

# Dedication

To, Our Children and Grandchildren
Thank you for your love and support.

Love,
Sharon and Terri

*"You know full well as I do the value of sister's affection. There is nothing like it in this world."*

-

Charlotte Bronte-

## Chapter One

The rain was falling on Thursday night as Montana Castle, private detective and security, pulls into a parking place in front of The Shetland Art Museum.

She had arranged to meet Brent Mathews to transfer a relic, a jeweled cross, from Rome. The pitter patter of the raindrops on her umbrella echoed with the tapping of the heels of her boots on the wet pavement. The museum was lit up. The lobby lights, reflecting through the double glass doors, direct her path. Closing her umbrella with one hand, she pushes through the double door into the foyer.

Nodding at the second shift security guard, Ray Jones, she says, "Hi, Ray, it's sure is wet outside!"

"Not fit for man, nor beast." He laughs. "What can I do for you tonight Montana?"

"Have you seen Brent Mathews tonight? I am to meet him here at 9:00."

"Yes, he came in at 8:15 and told me he was to meet you at 9:00. He said to let you know he was going for coffee and would be back at 9:00. "Then he adds," Why don't you stay here out of the rain. I'm sure he'll be back."

Placing her umbrella in the umbrella stand by the desk, she smiles and says, "Thanks. I will wait here. I'll make myself comfortable in the chair by the window."

While she's waiting, she watches the raindrops fall on the sidewalk and remembers. Meeting Christopher Castle at the local college. They both had majored in forensic science and criminal law. After graduation, they joined the police academy and both were hired at Whispering Key Police Department. Working their way up through the ranks, they took the Lt. test and were promoted. They were partners and then a couple.

On their wedding day, Christopher gave her Castlekeep Ridge as a wedding present. During the next three years, they filled the cabin with lots of memories. One rainy night, just like this one, they were called to a hostage situation. As the hours passed a shot echoed in the stillness, and found its target in her right thigh. Christopher, seeing she was hit, left his place of cover, and belly crawled to her side.

As he reached her, he lifted up and a bullet exploded through his back. In horror she watched as blood flowed from his chest, screaming, "Cop down." She dragged herself to his side and held him as he died, his pain-filled eyes reflecting their love.

Coming back to the present and glancing down at her watch, she sees it's 9:15. Standing up, she approaches Ray at the desk and asks, "Have you seen him yet?"

"No, his car is still out there, maybe he's still at the coffee house."

"Well, I better go check, thanks again. See you soon."

Closing the door behind her, she opens the umbrella, and walks to The Artistic License Coffee House. Seeking a warm latte, she enters and orders from Mary Smith at the counter. "Hi, Mary, I'm sooo cold. I need a warm latte, hold the topping."

Mary smiles and says, "Hi, Montana! It will be right up."

Looking around, Montana asks, "Did you see Brent Mathews in here tonight? I was supposed to meet him but I guess we got our wires crossed."

"Yes, he came in around 8:15, 8:30 or so."

"When did he leave?"

Handing Montana the latte, Mary says, "He left with another guy, who had been waiting for him. I guess it was around 9:00 they got up and left."

"Brent and the other guy?"

"Yes, they left together."

Taking her latte, and smiling at Mary she asks, "Was it David Thomas?"

"No it wasn't David. I haven't seen this guy before."

"Well, I guess I've been stood up." Leaving the coffee house, she scans the area to see if he's waiting, and notices his rental, a late-model, dark Toyota Camry, was gone.

******

The sunshine streams through the lacy curtains and the gentle morning breeze tickles Shannon Trevor's nose as she wakes up on this Friday morning. She had a restless night and nightmares she couldn't recall. Glancing over to her French clock, she sees that the time is later then she liked. Grabbing her robe and slipping into her slippers, she hurries downstairs to see if Wayne had gone.

Running into the kitchen, she sees the note he's left, picks it up, and reads:

*You tossed and turned all night. So I thought I'd let you sleep. Coffee is made, and I have business meetings all day. So I'll try to catch you later. Did Brent stop by and pick up the key last night? I know he was supposed to, but I didn't see him. Looking forward to getting together with him this Sunday for dinner at the country club with our friends before the relic display. I better go, have a good day. I'll see you tonight. Love ya, sweet pea.*

Pocketing the note in her robe, Shannon pours a mug of coffee and climbs up the stairs to get ready for her day. I wonder why we haven't heard from him? Maybe I'll call his folks and see if he's there, after I get to work.

After she's ready, Shannon returns to the kitchen and removes the tray of chocolate chip scones from the pantry and carries them out to her cream and brown Volkswagen Beetle. Opening the trunk, she lays them inside and closes it. Then, returning to the red brick and white Cape Cod style house, she gathers her clutch, laptop, and briefcase, and carries them out to the car, locking the door behind her. Singing along with a CD she arrives at Trevor Travels, her travel agency, and pulls into her designated parking place.

Carrying her briefcase, and lap top, she opens the beveled door, and enters into the foyer. Walking through the Queen Anne style sitting room, she enters her office, and places her lap top, and briefcase, on her Queen Anne style oak writing desk. Returning to the Beetle, she opens the trunk, and carries the tray of scones into the kitchenette, and lays them on the counter. Tapping fresh- ground coffee beans, into the basket she starts the coffee.

She again wonders why Brent hadn't called. When Brent Mathews called her earlier, she was surprised to hear from him. He was bringing a relic for the upcoming art exhibit on Sunday and happily added his name to the trip for tomorrow's tour group. He was to meet Montana last night to transfer the jeweled cross. He had been a lifelong friend of her husband, Wayne, and they were looking forward to seeing him again. They were planning on getting together for dinner with their friends before the relic exhibit.

The coffeemaker beeped and she poured a mug and inhaled the deep, roasted aroma. Thinking of Brent, she remembers the friendship the three of them shared. So many memories, each of them a precious treasure, to open and relish time after time. The grandfather clock in the sitting room, rang out the hour, and she knew Chloe Hope and Montana Castle would be here soon.

Carrying her coffee into the office, she opens her planner, and reviews the plans for the trip tomorrow. Booting up her computer, she finishes her coffee, and opens the itinerary for the bus trip to Gator Cove Casino. As the clock chimes the half hour, she stands, returns to the kitchenette, and places her cup on the counter. Gathering the trash, she ties the bag, and humming, heads for the dumpster. Suddenly she drops the bag and stifles a scream. Running over to the rain-soaked man lying on the ground, she hesitates, then squats down. With a gasp of recognition, she jumps back up and staggers through the door into the kitchen.

Quickly slamming the door with her foot, she wrings her hands and wraps her arms around her trembling body. Running to the office, she grabs her cell and dials 911.

Pacing the floor and knowing her sisters should be on their way, she dials her cell and tries to reach Wayne. When he doesn't answer she decides to call him later. Pouring another mug of coffee, she hurries into the sitting room, and sits down on a blue brocade Queen Anne wingback chair. Tapping her feet and crossing and uncrossing her slender legs, she nervously wonders what's keeping her sisters and the police? Looking at her pale face and dark curls in the antique gild framed mirror, she shivers. She does not want to be alone...she trembles and thinks she's not alone...someone is near, she can feel it. Taking another sip of the warm brew, she glances up at the copy of a painting of a seaside village in France by Monet...usually it calms her, not today...not this time.

Nervously she waits. In only a few minutes, it seems like hours, she hears the tinkle of the front door bell. Looking up, she sees her two sisters, laughing as they enter the agency. Seeing her pale face, they rush over. Montana, a PI, squats down, and removes the mug from her sister's cold hands, and takes hold of them with her two warm ones.

Chloe stoops down too, and as they both search her face, Montana asks, "Hey, big sis, how are you doing? You look a fright. Tell us what happened?"

"Yes, what happened to make you look like death warmed over, Shannon?"

Timidly, Shannon smiles at her older sister and answers Chloe, "You sure know how to make a girl feel good. "Then, looking at her younger sister adds, "I think Brent Mathews is outside lying by the dumpster. I took out the trash this morning and saw him."

Shaking her head and with tear- filled eyes asks, "Montana, did you meet with him last night to secure the relic?"

Montana, looking from Chloe to Shannon, answers, "I was to meet him at the Shetland Art Museum. He didn't show. The guard said he went for coffee. So I went to Artistic License Coffee House and spoke with Mary Smith .She said he left with a man who met him there. Did you call 911?"

Shannon nods, picks up her mug from the coffee table, takes another swallow, stands up, leads her two sisters out the back door and gestures for them to go ahead. While she waits, she wrings her hands and looks around, avoiding looking at Brent's still body.

Chloe, running to his side, turns and asks over her shoulder, "Montana, do you think we need to roll him over for proper identification?"

Shaking her head, Montana answers, "No, Chloe. We should wait for Chief Blake. I'm sure he'll be here soon. I hear the sirens in the distance."

Chloe pulls her Minolta from beneath her olive jacket and snaps pictures of the scene. Squatting down, she gently rolls him over and stares into the sightless blue eyes of her friend. Stumbling back as she rises, she begins to back into her sisters and says pointing, "That *is* Brent Mathews! *It is* Brent Mathews! *He's* not breathing! What happened?"

Suddenly the sirens are closer and the blue strobe lights fill the front of the building. The sound of running feet is heard, as Chief Steve Blake runs around the corner of the building and sees the three sisters, rushes over and says, "Is everyone okay?" The three women nod and, looking around, he says, "This is a crime scene, and you girls need to return to the agency. I'm going to get the yellow tape, I'll see you inside."

Montana, Chloe and Shannon walk slowly back into the kitchenette and Montana tells her sisters, "You girls go into the sitting room, and I'll bring coffee. "Then, looking at them both, asks, "Or would you like tea?"

"Coffee is what I need, Shannon?" Chloe says, shivering with grief.

"Coffee for me too. My mug is on the counter." Shannon tells her.

Devastated, the two girls return to the sitting room and, sitting down together on the rose brocade sofa, slowly lean back and sigh. Tears flow as the two sisters realize the sad loss of their friend outside. Montana enters and hands each girl a mug of the strong, roasted brew. Then sitting down on the blue wing back chair, takes a drink of her coffee. Reaching for the box of tissue on the table, she hands them to her sisters and together, the three sit in silence. Looking out the beveled window, they see the forensic team and the coroner arrive. The mumbled sound of voices can be heard through the walls. Slowly, the girls begin reminiscing about Brent.

Half an hour later, Chief Blake returns from the crime scene and tells them, "We're done here, Shannon. Which one of you turned him over? His shirt wasn't as wet as it should have been if he fell that way. You know you can be in trouble for disturbing the scene. I'll need your statements down at the station today. Montana, tell them what they need to do. I'm on my way to his folk's house, so I won't be at the station when you get there." Bending down to face Shannon, he pats her hands, which are folded in her lap, smiles softly, and says, "I don't think you'll want to stay here today. We'll have everything out of here tonight so you won't have to worry about tomorrow. Wish we could have joined you, I'm told," smiling at Montana, "that it's a lot of fun with the tour group. Maybe we can join you on the next tour." Standing up, he looks across at Montana. "Babe, did you meet Brent last night as arranged?"

Montana, glancing up at him says, "No, babe, I didn't. You were asleep last night when got back home so I didn't tell you. Why?"

Running his hands through his salt and pepper hair and placing his hands on his slender hips, he tells her, "There was an empty briefcase lying near him. If you didn't get the relic, then it's gone."

Shaking his head once more, he strides into the kitchenette and the sound of a closing door echoes in the room.

Soon the silence surrounds them again and Montana rises and takes the mugs for refills, saying, "I'll get refills, girls. I see you brought chocolate chip scones for us this morning, Shannon. Sorry I'm going to miss our coffee time this morning. Mind if I grab one on my way out? Is this Grandma Belle's recipe?"

Smiling, Shannon says, "Yes, yes it is. I think it's one of all our favorites. Do you girls remember the tea parties we shared with Grandma Belle?"

The girls share a smile, remembering, and Chloe, gesturing to the oak and crystal fronted Queen Anne style display cabinet says, "Those are the teacups and teapots we used when we learned the fine art of teatime. When other kids were hearing fairytales and nursery rhymes, we were taught family history and etiquette. Each cup and teapot told a story."

The three sisters share a smile, then Montana takes the mugs to the kitchenette, and within minutes, returns with a tray of scones, plates, napkins, Devonshire cream and two mugs of coffee. Grabbing a napkin and scone, she says, "Well, I better walk over to David's office at the art museum." Waving bye with a mouthful of scone she leaves.

Chloe and Shannon sit back and share more memories of their school friend, Brent Mathews. Time slips away.

******

Steve Blake looks over at the two story blue and brick colonial home. It is still morning, and as he parks, he thinks this is the hardest part of my job as an officer of the law. He shakes his head, and climbing out of his white Ford Ranger, he walks up to the door and rings the doorbell. Removing his hat as the door is opened, he smiles, and greets the white- haired matronly woman on the other side of the storm door.

She opens the door and invites him into her home. "Well, Chief Blake, what brings you here? Are you out gathering donations again?" She smiles.

"Uh, no, Miss Mary, is the Doc here?"

Turning as the tall silver-haired gentleman comes from the outside patio door, Steve puts out his hand, after shaking it, Dr. Mike offers, "We were just having our breakfast out on the patio. Would you like a cup of coffee?"

"Sure, thanks."

Together, the two men exit the patio door, and Mary returns to the kitchen to get another cup and saucer.

After accepting a cup of coffee, Steve takes a sip and, returning it to the saucer, tells them. "You know, there is no easy way to say this, but I need to let you know that Brent was killed either early this morning or late last night. I won't know for sure until after the autopsy. But it looks like it was a robbery as well. The relic he was delivering to the art museum was taken. When did you two see or talk with him last?"

As tears of grief and sorrow rock his wife's body, Mike takes her hand and tightens his arm around her, he soothes her like a mother with a startled baby, rocking her slowly and letting her cry tears of pain, sorrow, emptiness and grief.

Looking over at Steve he tells him, "Chief, we haven't seen him lately. He was planning on coming for a visit but had some business to take care of first. I think he said he was delivering a relic to the museum and he would see us after he delivered it. To be honest, Chief, I didn't think we'd see him until Sunday."

Taking a ragged breath, Mary says, "Yes, Sunday. I had talked to him just last night, Thursday evening, about 8:00 o'clock. He said he had checked in at the Lamplighter Inn, but would be over for Sunday dinner at1:00 o'clock."

"I hate to ask, but why not here?"

"I can tell you, Chief. Mary may not have known. I spoke to him a couple of weeks ago, he let me know he was coming to deliver the relic. He also said he didn't want to impose on us. He mentioned he may stay with Shannon and Wayne. She has that apartment above her agency. I guess he's been told he could stay there if he wanted to, when he came for a visit."

Wiping her eyes with her napkin, Mary adds, "They've both been his dear friends." Smiling, she continues, "He had dated her, Chief, through high school and college. He even worked with her while she was working at the art museum. But when her folks died, he accepted an internship with a school in Rome and left the scene. He left the field open for Wayne. He was their best man and best friend."

"Well, Doc, Miss Mary, I need to go. Let me know, if I can do anything for you. I am really sorry to have to bring you this kind of news."

Standing up and placing his hat back on his head, he turns and leaves. When he reaches the front of the house, he looks back, and notices both are crying.

******

Montana dusts her fingers on the napkin and strides across the street to the Shetland Art Museum. The museum had been hit by a hurricane and had recently been completely renovated. The Whispering Key Historic Society kept close to the original design. The addition of a painted, fiberglass horse in honor of the event stood beside the gateway to the floral garden that surrounded the museum. The fragrance of the garden envelopes her and the morning breeze gently lifts her golden- brown hair. Pushing open the glass door, Montana enters the cool foyer and approaches the receptionist at the desk.

The white- haired, small lady welcomes her and asks, "Montana, how are you?"

"Oh, fine, I guess, Miss Florence. Is David in yet?"

"I think he is, let me check." Florence picks up the phone and calls David Thomas, the museum curator. Then, turning back to Montana, smiles and says, "He's been waiting for you. He said you were bringing the relic." Montana lifts her empty hands and shakes her head Realizing Montana didn't have it, Florence quickly adds, "Go on in."

Smiling her thanks, Montana climbs the stairs to his office. Knocking on the door at the top of the stairs, he beckons her to come in, and stands as she enters.

"Good morning, Montana. I was anxious about this relic… is something wrong, I don't see it?" Sitting down, he rubs his hands down his face, and rests his chin in his one hand and drums the fingers of his other hand on the desk, he says, "Please sit down, and tell me what happened."

Sitting down in a chair across from him, Montana moves forward and tells him, "No, David, I didn't bring the relic, because I did not get it. I was to meet Brent last night, he didn't show. I'm sorry, but that's not all the bad news I have for you either."

Dropping his hands to his lap, he pulls closer to his desk, sighs and says, "Go ahead, Montana. Was there an accident? Will he be okay? Where is the relic?"

"Well, no accident, David. Shannon found him dead behind her office this morning when she took out the garbage and more bad news, the relic was stolen. I'm not sure, I don't have all the details yet, but it appears he was attacked from behind."

"Poor Shannon. She and Wayne have been friends with Brent Mathews for a long time. He was good friends with them both. He was even their best man." Shaking his head in sorrow, he adds, "She must be devastated." Looking across his desk with grief-filled, blue eyes, and running his fingers through his thick white hair, he adds, "How is she doing?"

"Oh, she'll be fine. She had a terrible shock. Finding someone dead is not a pleasant thing...and well, someone she knew ..." Standing up, she tells him, "I'm sure Steve will keep you posted. He's going to have to make some calls, but he'll keep you aware of the investigation. I better get down to my office. I have some paperwork to complete."

"Montana, "He calls her, as she reaches the door and she turns toward him, he adds, "Do you think this has anything to do with that group of robberies Patrick Reagan has been investigating?"

Looking at him, she replies, "I don't know, David. Could you call Emilee and let her know? I'm sure she'll want to call Shannon."

"Yes, I will, Montana."

As she closes the door, she hears David on the phone to his wife. Montana waves goodbye to the receptionist and walks across the street to her Jeep and drives the few blocks to her business, Black Widow Private Investigation and Gun Shop. She enters and makes a pot of coffee. This is going to be a busy day. While the coffee brews she thinks, yes, she knows grief too. She pours a cup, and taking her coffee to her desk, she looks at the picture of Chief Steve Blake. They had been dating exclusively, and were living together in her cabin at Castlekeep Ridge. Sitting down at her computer, she continues on her current investigation of the recent art robberies, she had agreed to help the FBI. Her sources said there had been four, now, this is number five. What is this all about? Could this be part of the same crime? A murder, too?"

******

As Montana left, David dialed his home phone and Emilee answered. "Thomas residence, this is Emilee here, can I help you?"

"Yes, Emilee, it's me. I just heard some heart-stopping news. Brent Mathews was found dead this morning behind Shannon's agency."

"Oh, no! That is terrible! Have you talked to Shannon?"

"No, dear. Montana just left here. Also, the relic is gone."

"The relic, oh dear, that is very disturbing news. Did she tell you anything else?"

"No, everything is under wraps right now. I was told, though she assured me, Steve would keep me informed."

"Well, I better get off here, I'm going to try to call Shannon. I'll see you tonight. Okay? We're having company for dinner, don't forget."

"Okay. I'm glad you reminded me, my dear. I, more than likely, would be late, and that's never good manners."

"No, no dear, it's not." Sadly, she hangs up. Quickly dialing Shannon's cell phone, she anxiously paces the floor waiting for an answer. Shannon, arriving at the police station, answers the music tone, alerting her it was Emilee Thomas. "Hi, Emilee. I'm glad you called, but, can I call you later?"

"Oh, of course, I just wanted to let you know David spoke to Montana and told me about Brent Mathews. I am so sorry. I know you and Wayne must really be grieving right now."

"Actually, Emilee, I haven't told Wayne yet. I tried earlier but couldn't reach him. I'll try again after I get this over with. I'm at the police station to give my statement. Oh, Emilee, I am so devastated. The loss of our friend has touched me deeply."

"Oh, I know sweetie, but they'll find out who did this. I know you will get your head back on right and do it yourself if they don't. I remember how we worked on that weekly paper in high school and you had a nose for investigating. Just breathe slowly and you'll be ok .call me later, okay?"

"Sure will, Emilee. Bye for now."

Closing her phone and placing it on silent, she places it in her clutch, and climbs out of her cream and brown Beetle convertible. Chloe had parked her burgundy Miata convertible next to her Beetle and was waiting at the door of the police station. When they finished giving their statements, about the mornings events, they were planning on baking at Chloe's. High calorie stress relief. Shannon smiles.

The two sisters enter the police station and are greeted by Officer Mike O'Rourke. He is a giant of a man.

Standing up at the desk, he approaches them and smiles. "Here for your statements ladies?"

Nodding, Chloe says, "Yes, let's get this over with."

Stroking his fingers along his goatee, he leads the girls to separate interrogation rooms. "Shannon, you wait in here, and I'll have Officer Randy Lewis help you with your report."

Shannon enters the room and takes a seat at the table. "Thanks, Officer O'Rourke." She looks up and smiles warily at him, "Yes, let's get this over with."

"And you, my dear Chloe, can come right this way, we'll put you in this cozy room, and I'll be right back."

"I can hardly wait." Chloe passes in front of him and enters the interrogation room.

Officer Randy Lewis knocks and enters the room, smiling at Shannon. It had been a long time since she had seen him. Her son, Zachary, and he were friends during school. She and Wayne had joined his parents for many sports and church activities. He was in good shape and had shaggy, blond hair and laughing, blue eyes.

"It's been a long time, Mrs. Trevor. Sorry to get together under these circumstances. Before we begin, can I get you anything to drink?"

"A glass of water would be nice."

Returning with the water, he sits down across from her and says, "Now to begin, I would like you to tell me everything that occurred after you arrived at your agency."

Shannon trembles as she remembers the blank look of Brent's eyes...such a loss...he was so young. "Well, Wayne and I had invited Brent to stay at the apartment upstairs above the agency. He was going to join us on our trip tomorrow."

"Trip?"

"Yes, the bus tour to Gator Cove Casino. He didn't stop by last night for the key, and never called."

"So you haven't talked with him since, when did you speak last?"

"It was early this week, maybe Monday or Tuesday."

"So he never called or contacted you or Wayne since?"

"No. This morning I overslept and Wayne was already gone when I got up. He left a note saying he hadn't seen Brent either. I gathered the scones I had baked last night and loaded them into my car. Then I drove to work."

"What did you do when you got to work?"

"I made coffee and checked over the itinerary for the trip tomorrow. I went back to my office to do that about 7:00. The grandfather clock struck seven times. I worked about half an hour, went for a second cup of coffee, and set up for our Friday Coffee. My sisters and I meet at my agency every Friday at 8:00."

"So you made coffee, you worked on the trip, and then what happened?"

"I gathered the garbage to take out to the dumpster...that's when I found Brent...Brent Mathews, he was lying beside the dumpster."

"Did you touch the body or check for life?"

"No...no...I backed up into my door and returned to the kitchenette."

"When did you call 911?"

"Well, shortly after that, I was upset and restless. I sat down and waited for my sisters to arrive."

"The 911 call was noted at 7:45 and they arrived at 7:50. Did you return to the scene before they arrived?"

"Yes, I did. When my sisters arrived we...I took them out there. I couldn't even look at him. I was so upset. I...I"

"It's okay, Mrs. Trevor. But what did your sisters do?"

"Well, I remember that Chloe asked Montana, if they should roll him over for proper identification. And, of course, Montana told her no. But, well, Chloe didn't listen. She's impulsive and wanted to make sure he was gone."

"When Chief Blake arrived, what happened?"

"He sent us back into the agency while he and his team secured the scene."

"Anything else, Mrs. Trevor, you want to add?" Shaking her head no, he continues, "Well, I'm going to type this up and bring it back in for your signature. Do you want anything while you are waiting?"

"No, I'll be fine. Thanks, Randy."

*****

As Chloe waits for Officer O'Rourke, she becomes impatient. Drumming her fingers on the table and looking at her watch, she stands and begins to pace in the small room. Her pace is halted by a knock on the door.

"Mrs.. Hope, I'm Officer Robin Lee. I understand you're here to give a statement. I'm sorry you had to wait...there was a little confusion out there. I thought Officer O'Rourke was going to speak with you, but... well, sometimes...you don't have to worry about that. Anyway, here is the form and this won't take long."

Chloe smiles in relief and sits back down. She had known Robin Lee from her daughter's class. They had both been involved in girls' basketball, soccer and cheerleading. Later, she had been one of Montana's prize students, and was an avid horsewoman. She had grown into a beautiful young woman. Nodding in approval, she thinks, yes, and she does wear her uniform well. She was slender and wore her long dark hair down and Chloe remembered her laughing, blue eyes, and smiling, she remembers the pranks the two girls got into.

"Well, it's been a long time, Robin. You have turned out well."

"Thanks, Mrs. Hope. I guess my reputation helped pave the way to my career." She smiles back, then adds, "Now let's get through this. You can begin when you arrived at Mrs. Trevor's agency."

"Well, Montana and I arrived at the agency at the same time. We were sharing a laugh about this morning at Montana's."

"So when you two entered, what did you see?"

"Well, Shannon was very pale, and we could tell, she wasn't her old self. She was frightened. We ran over to her, and Montana and I asked her what was wrong. I think we both were concerned that something happened to Wayne. We never dreamed it would be Brent Mathews."

"So did she tell you?"

"Yes, she said she thought she had found Brent Mathews out by the dumpster, we followed her out and that's when we saw him."

"You saw Mr. Brent Mathews? What did you and Mrs. Castle do?"

"Yes, it was Brent Mathews. I asked if we should roll him over and make sure he was dead."

"Did Mrs. Trevor call 911?"

"Yes, she had called. Montana told me I shouldn't disturb the scene, but well, I wanted to make sure, so I rolled him over."

"So you knew the police were on their way?"

"Well yes. Montana cautioned me not too."

"That wasn't a good idea, Mrs. Hope. I'll have to take your fingerprints, because they'll be on the body. Did you see anything that may be important for us?"

"No, just that there was a briefcase next to him. He was supposed to meet Montana last night and hand it over. But she said she never met him. She waited but he never showed."

"Okay, so anything else?"

"No, nothing else."

"Okay, have you ever had your fingerprints done, Mrs. Hope? It's not painful."

"Oh, yes, I have, Robin. As you know, my husband and I have a business. We raise and race harness horses. My prints are on file."

"Okay, would you care for something to drink, while I type this up? Coffee? Then I'll need your signature and you can go."

"Yes, coffee would be wonderful! Black, please. Thank you, Robin."

Robin returns with a cup of coffee and leaves to type up the statement.

*****

After completing their statements, Shannon and Chloe meet in the lobby.

Seeing Sgt. O'Rourke Shannon asks, "Officer, is there anything else?"

"No, girls, you're free to go, for now. If we have any questions, we'll call. "Then laughing, "You two don't plan on leaving the area soon, anytime soon now do you?"

Chloe stares at him with piercing, hazel eyes, "That is not funny!

Shannon, we better get out of here, before this clown gets me really crazy."

Officer O'Rourke laughs. Turning her back abruptly to him, she picks up her Coach bag, and Shannon picks up her small Rossetti clutch and says to Chloe, as they leave, "Now, Chloe, don't let him get to you. He's just trying to lighten the situation. At least, I think he is! Steve didn't say anything like that earlier, remember?"

"Yes, I do. "Then pointing her thumb over her shoulder says, "That character has always rubbed me the wrong way." Smiling wickedly at her sister, Shannon says, "Some men get off on seeing a woman's temper rise, do you want to share your secrets with meek, innocent, younger sister?"

"No, I don't. "Then laughing she says, "You couldn't handle it, my dear. That's why you have Wayne, and I have Tennessee."

Climbing into their cars, they take off and soon arrive at Chloe's home. Hope Ranch was a standard-bred horse ranch, with a half-mile training track where Tennessee Hope trained his horses for harness racing. Chloe also had established a darkroom in the house. Now with the growth in her business, she recently opened Chloe's Moments Studio. Most people assumed she had moved everything to her studio downtown. But she kept some equipment at home, too.

Chloe, slipping out of her jacket, hangs it on the coat tree inside her foyer. Taking the camera to the darkroom, she leaves it on the workbench. Returning to the kitchen after washing her hands, she dons an apron and begins gathering bowls, measuring cups, etc. for their baking this afternoon. Opening her homemade recipe noteboOkay, she locates the two recipes they had decided on for the coming bus trip tomorrow, Mini Cinnamon Rolls and Deep, Rich, Chocolate Brownies. Shannon washes up, too, dons an apron, and together they spend the afternoon relieving the stress from the earlier morning, at the discovery of Brent Mathews by enjoying the silence, and the comfortable aroma of chocolate and cinnamon, and a dose of hazelnut coffee too.

Removing the rolls from the state-of-the-art oven, Shannon places them on the counter to cool, while she mixes the cream cheese glaze. Chloe finishes mixing the rich and chocolaty batter, and pours the mixture in a prepared pan.

Sliding it in the oven, she turns, wiping her hands with a blue tea towel, suggests, "Let's have a cup of coffee and relax while we're waiting for the brownies to finish baking."

Shannon looks up from dribbling the glaze across the cinnamon rolls and agrees, "Sounds like coffee time to me."

Shannon, wiping her hands with a paper towel, takes a mug from the cabinet above the coffee maker and pours a cup of the hazelnut brew. Chloe, removing another mug, fills it and inhales the nutty aroma, then leads the way to the knotty pine table, pulls out a chair and sits down, then nodding to her sister says, "Take a sit, sister dear."

Shannon laughs, and pulling a chair out, sits down across from Chloe. Without fail, the conversation continues from earlier at the travel agency. "It's hard to believe he's gone, Chloe."

Sipping her coffee, Chloe nods and says, "Yes, it is. Were you talking to Wayne when we got to the police station?"

Shaking her head, Shannon says, "No, that was Emilee. She wanted to let me know she heard the news, and they wanted to let me know they shared in our sorrow."

"Don't you think you need to call him, Shannon?"

"Yes, I do. Perhaps I should wait until I see him tonight."

"Well, I know it won't be easy, but the sooner he is told, the better off, I think." Swallowing another drink from her mug, she says, "You're right, Chloe, as usual. I guess I'll try again now." Shannon stands and removes her cell phone from her purse and then looks over at Chloe. "I have a missed call, it's from Waync. I must not have turned it on after we left the police station. Oh, I hope he hasn't heard from someone else." Quickly she dials her husband on his cell and, again it's not answered. She then dials the office and, again, no answer. "Well, that's strange. He called me, but I can't seem to reach him. I guess I better finish up here, load the goodies, and then head home."

"Fine with me, I want to get those pics I took developed before Tennessee gets home. Do you remember if Montana saw me take them?"

Shaking her head, she says, "No, I can't say I was paying attention, Chloe. But you should let her see them. You're good with details, so maybe they might display something relevant."

"Oh, I will, Shannon. I forgot to check with you earlier, is everything ready for tomorrow?"

"Yes, I pick up the bus at 8:00, we'll have rolls and coffee and leave at 9:00. I hate to leave good company, but as for me, I'm going to be on my way. But I'm not going to let this go either. I want to find out who killed him. He should still be here going with us tomorrow, you know?"

Chloe hugs her sister and says, "He should have had more time. We'll solve this. I'll start with these pics. Now let me help you wrap these and load them in your car. I'll bring the brownies when I join you tomorrow, okay?"

Shannon says, "Yes, thanks again. I'll see you at 7:00."

While the brownies finish baking, Chloe sits down for another cup of coffee. She stretches out her long dancer's legs and thinks about Brent in high school. He was in band, and Wayne and him were the best of friends. They graduated and both of them chose to attend the same college, Florida State, and she attended a small college outside New York City.

Weekends were fun when they all got together, which was not often. She had received a full scholarship for photography and dance. She lived too far away for many weekends home, so she enjoyed the ballet, the plays, the concerts and modeled in fashion shows. She chuckled to herself, oh, but not the snow...the cold...she was a Florida girl through and through.

Upon graduation, she returned to Whispering Key and began her adult life. One weekend that summer she joined her friends Darrell and Trish Andrews for a harness race at Pompano Race Track. A former classmate and flame, Tennessee Hope met her there and won three races, and Chloe won his heart. They were together every day, and eventually she moved in with him at his ranch. Soon wedding bells rang out the news that they would be sharing the rest of their lives together. Memories were made between them and were still happening. She places her mug in the dishwasher and heads to her darkroom.

******

Chief Steve Blake looked down at the report on his desk, and standing walks around his desk and over to the window overlooking the hot and sullen street. A lifelong resident, and former lieutenant on the police force, shakes his salt and pepper head, strokes his salt and pepper beard, and reflects on the murder and robbery he is now responsible to clear. Returning to his desk, he sits back down and completes the preliminary report on Brent Mathews.

The phone rings and, picking up the receiver, he answers, "Yeah, Blake here."

"Steve, this is Ralph Andrews. I've completed the autopsy report on Brent Mathews. He died from a blow of a sharp metal object to the back of his head. I also found slivers of metal in the wound. I'm running tests on that, but it could be from the relic. He was negative for drugs and no sign on his hands of self-defense, like skin under the fingernails etc. I'm sure he knew his attacker, but was caught by surprise. My estimated time of death is approximately 9:30 p.m. Was there a security bracelet attached to the briefcase? He has a mark where the chain could have scratched his wrist."

As Steve ponders that, he tells Ralph, "We did not find a chain. Fax me the report. Thanks. Have a good night. "Twirling a pencil in his hand, he waits for the report, upon receiving it, he decides to return Montana's call.

# Chapter Two

Chloe stands beside the work table in the dark room, completing the final wash of the photos she had taken at the crime scene. As images appear on the paper, she watches and remembers the blank stare of Brent's lifeless eyes. Then she sees it, a piece of chain that had been attached to Brent's wrist, lying beside his body, and a gold ring with a black crest. Murmuring under her breath, 'Of course, that would be the security chain attaching the briefcase to Brent's wrist, however the chain is not on the briefcase. But what is that ring?' She finishes processing the rest of the photos, hanging them up to dry on clips on the line above her head. She puts away the chemicals and washes her hands.

Before leaving the darkroom, she picks up her cell phone from the worktable and speed dials Montana. Excitedly, "I just developed the pictures I took this morning. Do you remember a broken chain attached to Brent's wrist?" Hurriedly adding, "There was also a shiny object and so I enlarged that frame. It is a gold ring with a black crest like the fraternity ring Brent always wore."

"It could have been a robbery gone bad. I would like a copy of those pics. I'll call Steve and see what I can get out of him. Can you drop off the pics on your way in town tomorrow?"

******

Returning to the kitchen, she sees Tennessee standing at the counter, he says, "Hi, sweetie, what's for dinner?" Walking over to him, she kisses him softly on the lips and suggest, "How about Chinese?"

Tennessee agrees, and goes over to the phone and dials Shrimp & Seafood Buffet, ordering their supper. He joins Chloe on the suede, tan sectional and asks her, "How was your day, babe?"

Chloe snuggles close to Tennessee and sadly, tells him, "I have to tell you what happened today. Shannon found Brent Mathews lying dead beside her dumpster."

Wrapping Chloe in his arms, he asks, "Brent Mathews was in our class, wasn't he?"

"Yes, he was." Chloe continues, "Before Steve arrived, I took photos of the scene. I just developed them, and guess what?"

Startled, Tennessee stands up and begins pacing. Turning to her, he asks, "What did you find?"

Chloe rises from the sectional and walks over to Tennessee. Taking his two calloused hands in her soft ones, squeezes his hands and says, "I found, in the photo, a chain and a black and gold crest ring, lying beside his body."

The doorbell rings, interrupting their conversation, announcing the arrival of their food. Tennessee reaches in his jeans for cash and pays the delivery man. Closing the door, he returns to the family room, places the food on the coffee table, and joins Chloe on the sofa.

"How's Broadway doing today?" Chloe asks.

"Poor thing, she's so miserable. She should foul any day. I'm keeping a close eye on her in case she needs help."

Opening the containers, the hungry couple, pick up their chopsticks and begin to devour the rice and vegetables. Swallowing after a few bites, Chloe places the Chinese container on the coffee table, turns sideways to face Tennessee, sits on her feet and animatedly tells him the rest of the details of her day.

******

Chief Blake closes the file he has been reading, picks up his cell phone and calls Montana. "Hi, babe! What are you doing?"

"I'm cleaning stalls. I could use an extra pair of hands." She chuckles into the phone, "What are you do in'?"

"I just got the autopsy report. Brent was killed by a blow to his head, and negative for drugs and alcohol. Did you happen to see a chain on the ground this morning? Ralph found scratches on his wrist but no chain."

"No, I didn't...Uh, what about the briefcase? Was a chain attached to the handle?"

"The briefcase had only the authenticity papers, no relic and no chain on the handle."

"Okay...the motive is robbery. Were you able to lift prints?"

Steve replies, "Yes, Brent's and another unidentified print. I'm cross-checking with Rome on that one, it may be from the curator there. Are you planning to come back into town for supper or should I bring something home?"

"I have to finish here, could you bring something home?"

"Okay, I'll stop by Roger's and pick up ribs and slaw. See you later, love ya babe."

Montana smiles, and says, "Me too! See ya later."

She lifts another pitchfork of fresh straw and scatters it in Penny's stall. Checking all three stalls she fills the feed bucket and puts fresh water in the water buckets. Taking an apple slice from her shirt pocket, she lets Penny take it from the palm of her hand. Locking her stall, she goes to Goldie and Blaze's stalls and gives each a slice of apple and leaves the barn.

Heading for the cabin, she thinks, I need a bath and a change of clothes. Inside, she gets ready for a bubble bath, climbs in, and relaxes in an herbal/floral blend of bubbles, thoughts of the day jumble her mind. She wonders, could there have been another set of eyes watching us and waiting for us to go back inside? Did he see Chloe snap those pics? She climbs out of the tub and dries off with a soft, cream towel, and wraps herself in her favorite pink robe. Going into her bedroom, she sits on her bed. She glances at the picture hanging above her bed, one that Chloe had taken of Penny and her two babies, Blaze and Goldie, at dusk, standing along the river bank.

Montana goes to her closet and takes out a pair of jeans and a peach t-shirt. After dressing, she brushes her shoulder-length, golden brown hair, thinking, I need to get my highlights redone. I better call Trish and see if I can get in tomorrow. Going into the kitchen, she reaches for a glass from the knotty pine cupboard above the sink. Taking her glass to the side- by- side refrigerator, she fills it with ice from the door and takes a can of diet Coke from the fridge.

Sitting at the knotty pine kitchen table she reaches for the phone to call Trish . "Hello, this is Trish. How can I help you today?"

"Trish, this is Montana, hi. I was wondering how busy you are tomorrow? I need to get my highlights redone, can you work me in?"

Trish replies, "You're not going on the tour with your sisters tomorrow? I know you like to go up to the casino when they take a tour there."

Running her left hand through her hair, Montana says, "No, not this time. Steve and I have plans. We are going out to the Second Chance Ranch to set up a program for those kids tomorrow afternoon. That's why I wanted to see about tomorrow morning. How's your schedule?"

Looking at her appointment boOkay, Trish answers, "Well, I am open all morning, what is your pleasure? Do you want early or mid-morning?"

"How about 10:00? We usually go out for breakfast on Saturday morning, so we should be done by then, is that okay?"

"That will be fine, hon, see you then. "Trish hangs up the phone.

******

As Shannon is preparing the spinach salad, the kitchen phone rings. Cradling the phone between her ear and her shoulder, she continues to chop and answers, "Hi, Wayne, are you running late?"

"No, just meetings all day. Sorry I missed your call. What's up?"

Laying the knife on the cutting board, she sits down, wipes her hands and tells him, "Oh, Wayne, I have bad news to share. Brent Mathews is dead."

"Oh no, how? An accident?"

"No, I don't believe it was an accident. I found him by the dumpster at the agency this morning?"

"Oh, no! How are you holding up?"

"Moment by moment. I know Steve paid a visit to the Mathews, but perhaps you should call them too."

"Okay, I will before I leave here. Then I'll be home."

Pulling the phone toward him, he dials the familiar number. He watches the sky outside fading into evening twilight. Stars begin to light the smoky gray sky. Streetlights come on and he's certain many families are discussing their days.

Doc answers the phone and Wayne greets him and Miss Mary, "Hey, Shannon just gave the sad news. How are you two holding up? Is there anything I can do?"

"Oh, thanks, Wayne, there's so much still to be done. Mary and I would like to ask you about reading the eulogy? You're the one who knew him the best. I...I uh.. ..know he'd like that."

"Of, course, Doc. I'd be proud to. Thanks for asking."

The two continued reminiscing and, finally, Wayne hangs up after suggesting they get together for a round of golf. Now I have to get home. Turning out the lights, he locks up and leaves for home.

******

Shannon is removing the turkey enchiladas she was baking from the wall oven. The lights were coming on in her neighborhood. She knew Wayne would be home soon. She thought, hope not too long. Setting out the salad on the table, she lights the taper candles, and fills the sparkling glasses with water and lemon. Hearing Wayne come into the red and white kitchen, and dropping his keys on the marble counter beside her workstation, she smiles at him. The citrus scent of the salad of spinach leaves, mandarin oranges, and cheesy jalapeno and Mexican spices of the enchiladas, tantalizes his senses, his mouth waters in anticipation.

Coming up behind his wife, he nuzzles her neck and asks, "You seem lost in thought."

Leaning back against his chest, Shannon sighs and tells him, "Yes, I was thinking about our friend Brent. I had a trying day. How did your day go?"

"The meeting with the planning commission was long but was very informative. Maybe a glass of Chardonnay will relax you. I'll go get a wine glass for you, and make a Windsor and water over ice for me." Wayne says.

Shannon smiles at him and tells him, "Thanks, that would be great. Dinner is ready, so don't be too long, okay?"

Leaving the kitchen, Wayne tells her, "I won't be long. I'll be back in a flash."

Reaching the den, Wayne prepares his drink and takes a wine glass from the oak cabinet, turning to return to the kitchen. The desk phone rings and, as he reaches for it, tells her, "I'll get it, Shannon." Sitting down at the desk, he picks up the receiver, and says into the phone, "Hello, Wayne here."

"Hi, Wayne, this is Mike Phillips. I'm having dinner at Roger's BBQ and I ran into my informant from the police department."

"Some breaking news, Mike? Can't it wait? Shannon's holding supper for me."

"Have you spoken to Shannon about what happened down at her agency this morning? My informant told me Shannon and her sisters found a body back by the dumpster."

Wayne leans back in his chair and says, "Yes, we've talked."

"Do you want to meet me at the newspaper office after dinner? I have an angle I 'd like to talk about." Mike says.

"Sure, it sounds good, see you later. "Taking a long swallow of his drink, he stands up and mixes another, picking up her wine glass, he returns to the kitchen. He sees Shannon has taken her place at the table.

Shannon looks up and, seeing the tired look on his face, says, "Bad news?"

Walking over to the refrigerator, he pours wine into her glass and places it in front of her at the table. Sitting down across from her, he says, "That was Mike, he wants to meet at the office, to put the story about Brent in the early edition. He has spoken to his informant from the police department and has an angle he wants to pursue."

Shannon takes a drink of her wine and swallows, "Let's eat dinner so you can go."

Wayne looks at his wife and asks, "Does Steve have any leads yet?"

"I don't think so, he hasn't shared anything with us yet. Montana was supposed to meet Brent last night, but he didn't show. "Taking another sip of wine, she adds, "She was to receive a relic he was transporting from Rome, for the upcoming art exhibit this Sunday."

Finishing up their dinner, Wayne stands up and, taking his plate to the dishwasher, asks, "Do you need help with this?"

Shannon smiles, stands, kisses him and says, "No, thanks. I know you have things to do. I'll leave the light on. Love you."

Picking up his keys from the counter, he looks over at her, "Are you going to be okay, sweet pea?"

She walks up to him, and looks into his dark brown eyes . Wayne brushes her curls away from her face and caresses it. Searching her wide, dark eyes, he holds her face in his hands and then kisses her deeply. She watches him leave and, as his Charger roars and he drives away, she sighs and blows out the candles.

In the kitchen, she rinses the dishes and places them in the dishwasher. Turning around, she checks to see that everything is put away. She fills the deep apple- red teakettle, turns on the burner and places a Chamomile tea bag into a deep red mug. While the water is heating she goes into the laundry room and folds towels, and carries them up the stairs to the linen closet. Hearing the whistle from the teakettle, she returns to the kitchen, shuts off the burner and brews the mug of tea.

While the tea is brewing, she takes the warm mug in her cold hands and saunters into the living room. Sitting down in her sunny yellow rocker, she lifts the comforting and warm mug to her lips. Glancing above the fireplace, her eyes soften as she meditates on the copy of the Monet painting of a seaside village, her thoughts return to Brent...a sad ending.. for someone she worked with and knew over twenty-five years.

Finishing her tea, she takes the mug to the kitchen, rinses it and places it in the sink. Looking around once more, she locks the back door and turns off the kitchen light. Moving through the house she turns on the foyer light, and locking the front door, she climbs the stairs to her bedroom.

Deciding to take a warm relaxing bath with lavender bath oil, Shannon slides beneath the fragrant water, soaking and enjoying the lavender fragrance. Rising from the bath, she wraps in a thick towel and prepares for bed. Climbing into her four-poster maple bed, and sliding beneath the paisley and white quilt, she snuggles deep into the mattress and embraces much needed sleep.

******

Meanwhile at the Trevor Times, Wayne unlocks the door, and walks over to his dropping his keys in his pocket, he sits down at his desk, and reviews the AP wire. Mike Phillips comes in shortly after Wayne and stands at

Wayne's desk.

Mike runs his hand through his red hair and asks, "So, anything else that Shannon shared?"

"No, your informant was correct. The vic was Brent Mathews. She also told me that he was supposed to meet Montana to transfer a relic from Rome for an exhibit on Sunday. As you can guess, they didn't meet, he was a no-show. You know Mike, I knew Brent all my life."

"This must be hard on you both."

"Yes, it is, Mike. What did you want to do about another angle?"

Excitedly rising from his chair, he paces the floor and explains to Wayne. "What do you think about a bid for our readers to share stories on Brent Mathews?"

"This might be a good idea, Mike. Throughout the weekend, we can do stories on his life here at Whispering Key."

Mike looks over at Wayne and then says, "Great! I want to start with you. You were his best friend. Do you think you can allow me to interview you?"

"Oh, of course! Let's get started. I know it's going to be a late night. But, all of sudden, I don't feel so tired anymore."

******

The cell phone rings. Recognizing the number of his partner, he answers. "Yes, the plan went as expected, I have the relic."

"Good. Any witnesses?"

"No, I am going to check out a possible waitress. She is the only one who could identify him. It was dark in the coffee shop. It was a good night to put the plan into action, no folk, blues or jazz show on Thursday night."

"That's why we chose that place. Do you think she may be a problem?"

"No, I really don't think so. I'll keep my ears and eyes open, though. Like I said, it was dark in the coffee shop. I think it has to do with the atmosphere." He chuckles. "Well, I guess that's all for now. Keep this phone. It will be the only one I answer when you call. My home phone is not accessible for this business. Understand?"

"Of course, I wouldn't have it any other way. "The conversation ends.

******

The castle stood amidst the mountains. Built of stone and masonry, it had lasted through wars and generations of family residence. When he located it, it was after a tour of castles in Europe he had the chance to take, after his graduation from the college his father forced him to attend.

He remembered his father's words, "Make something of yourself, son. Have a plan and follow through."

Oh, he had learned it well. As he looked around his castle, his domain, he smiled as he stood up from the desk and pocketed his cell phone. Walking around the desk, his eyes feast on the treasures around and his short, stubby fingers caress them. That which he had, through his own ingenuity now possessed. Each treasure formerly owned by a famous museum in Europe and even in the Americas.

Walking over to his safe behind the antique, scarlet and gold tapestry-covered walls, he slides his fingers through the fake wall to release a lever, the wall opens where the safe is concealed. Turning the dial of the combination, he opens the safe where, inside, he views the jewels and money within, and reaching in, takes out the money pouch. Soon, I will meet my partner and exchange these unmarked bills for the relic the jeweled cross from Rome. Returning the pouch to the safe, he closes it and, as it clicks and locks, he laughs.

## Chapter Three

Awakening to the chimes of the tiny clock on the nightstand and the sunlight dancing Like fairy dust from the window, Shannon stretches and rolls over to see Wayne had not come to bed. Climbing out of bed, she slips on her robe and slippers and heads for the kitchen. Saturday had arrived, the day her tour group was going to Gator Cove Casino. The welcome aroma of coffee tickles her nose as she enters the kitchen filled with sunlight, promising a beautiful day. Passing the den, she sees that Wayne did come home, but it must have been really late. Wayne was sound asleep, covered with the multi-colored quilt she had made when they were first married.

Reaching the coffee pot, she pours a mug and gazes out the window above the sink. Looking out, she sees the rose covered arbor and white, picket fence enclosing the garden and the stone bench she enjoyed sitting on several times a week. She takes a sip and inhales the aroma. Hearing Wayne stir in the den, she fills another mug and hands it to him as he comes into the kitchen.

"Good morning, Wayne. Late night, huh? I am going to be having breakfast at the casino with the tour, there are bagels and fruit in the pantry and cream cheese and butter in the refrigerator."

"Got a lot accomplished. We're going to invite the community to send in stories of Brent. He interviewed me last night for this morning's intro."

Shannon reaches up and kisses him gently, and then, refilling her mug, says, "That sounds great, honey. I am sure the paper will get a lot of response. How will you be able to keep up with it?"

"Well, we're only having it until the funeral. By then, most who want to make a submission will have done so. I'm going to keep copies of the letters and make a book for his family."

Hugging Wayne, Shannon smiles up at him and says, "That sounds wonderful, Wayne. Will you be working today, too?"

"Yes, I have to. Mike is going to be checking with some folks he knows that knew Brent. Will you call me later about supper?"

"Sure, when we get back from the trip. Now, I better get upstairs to get dressed."

"Okay, I'll clean up here before I leave, Shannon. I'll also empty the dishwasher."

Dressing in a chocolate and ivory floral blouse and a pair of chocolate brown capris with a matching linen jacket, she chooses sterling silver hoop earrings and matching chain with an ivory cameo. Combing her chestnut curls and applying eye liner and lip gloss, and slipping on brown espadrilles, she picks up her brown, leather, hobo bag and heads down stairs.

Looking in the kitchen, she sees Wayne finishing up, and he says to her, "You look nice. Be careful. You know I love you."

"I love you, too, Wayne."

They kiss goodbye and Wayne turns back to get one more cup of coffee to go. Shannon leaves and heads for the agency.

******

As she is driving along and singing with a Martina McBride CD, suddenly, hitting her hands on the steering wheel, she remembers.

*How could I have forgotten about the security camera I installed on the back of my building at the agency, I need to check that out today, before Chloe gets here. It's good Chloe has to make a stop at Montana's first.*

Arriving at the agency, Shannon parks and carries the tray of cinnamon rolls into the agency. Laying them on the counter in the kitchenette, she opens the door to the staircase that leads to the apartment upstairs. She runs up the carpeted steps unlocks the door and enters the cozy two bedroom apartment. This was where Brent was invited to stay. She had stayed here before she married Wayne, she had purchased this building with her nest egg she saved during college. Here is where he surprised her on Christmas Eve, on bended knee...holding a heart-shaped, white velvet box...sliding the amethyst and black diamond, sterling ring...so many years ago...

Just a few days ago, she installed this motion detection, night- vision, dome camera by herself. Nobody knew she had done so, not Montana and not Steve. The only one who may know, well, she hoped not, would have been the killer. If he had somehow noticed it. It was designed to be inconspicuous, but some people notice things better than others. Then with all that happened yesterday, well, it slipped her mind. She hadn't even had a chance to see if she had installed it correctly. Now she would see if she had, and if it could shed some light on Brent's killer. Did she really want to see it before her eyes? Yes, she had to, and she had to tell Montana and Chloe.

Slowly the tape begins, she watches a bird's eye view of the back of her building. The tape shows the dumpster out by the alley, the cobblestone walk that leads from the back door to the dumpster and in shock she watches three figures. While the one on his left held a gun, the man on Brent's right removed a tool and clipped the chain from the briefcase. Then taking the briefcase, he opens it, unwraps the jeweled cross, and caresses it like she does a beloved book or her violin. She watches as the shorter man bludgeons Brent's head with the religious relic. Holding her breath she watches as her friend falls to the wet cobblestone sidewalk.

Leaving the scene, the two men back out, careful not to turn toward the camera. Yes, they knew about the camera. Glad she got it before they did, she had to share this with Montana and Chloe. Putting her face in her hands, tears fall down her cheeks, and through her fingers. The grandfather clock chimes in the sitting room, and she quickly washes her streaked face and places the tape in the zipped pocket of her purse with the key to the upstairs apartment.

She would wait until she had a chance to look at Chloe's photos.

Quickly, she locks the agency, briskly walks down to the parking garage, and collects her tour bus. The two sisters had been in business together for a few years, and now, with Chloe's Moments Studio opening, well, Chloe may not have time to continue the business with her. Chloe was rapidly building a clientele that Shannon knew was her sister's dream for many years. Chloe had provided photos for the tourists and now she was taking life's moments photos. Shannon was proud of her. Arriving back at the agency, she parks in front of the art museum. David had given her permission to park there on

Saturday morning. Downtown parking was free and the tourists knew it was also well-lit and the security that the museum provided assured that the cars would be safe.

Chloe pulls her Miata into the space next to Shannon's Beetle. She closes the door and locks the car. She straightens the solid, olive green top over the matching capris she is wearing and carries the tray of brownies into the agency. The multi-colored olive green scarf is wrapped once around her neck and the tails of the scarf flow down her back. Meeting Shannon at the door, they enter the travel agency and head for the kitchenette.

While Chloe prepares the cinnamon rolls for warming in the oven, she says, "I stopped by Montana's to drop off the pictures I took here yesterday morning."

Shannon, setting out napkins, forks, plates and cups, turns to Chloe as she starts the coffee, says, "How did they turn out?"

"You won't believe it!" she exclaims, "When I developed one frame, there beside Brent's body was a broken chain and a shiny object. I enlarged the image, centering on the chain, and you can see in the enlargement, that the shiny object is a gold ring with a black crest."

Shannon looks at Chloe and says, "When you rolled Brent over, didn't he have his fraternity ring on his right hand?"

Turning from the oven, and placing the hot cinnamon rolls onto a plate, Chloe stops, looks at Shannon and says, "Yes he did! I better call Montana." She speed dials Montana's number, no answer, so she leaves a message, "Montana, call me, I have more info about the ring!"

Loading trays with flaky cinnamon rolls and coffee, the sisters go out to the office to meet their guests. The air was filled with gossip and inquisitive chatter.

Ron and Betty Moore, accepting cinnamon rolls and coffee, Betty asks Shannon, "What happened here yesterday, we read in the Trevor Times that a body was discovered here?"

Before Shannon could reply, a small group gathers, she looks across the room at Chloe and says, "Yes, Brent Mathews was found here, the police are investigating so we can't discuss it."

Chloe interrupting, "More coffee, Ron? Betty?" Setting down her tray, Chloe says, "Time to board, folks."

Murmuring, the group places their plates, and cups in the trash container in front of the counter and board the bus.

******

Arriving at Gator Cove Casino, the tourists leave the bus and head into the lobby. While Chloe escorts them to the All-You-Can-Eat Brunch, Shannon walks over to the cashier's window to pick up the complimentary chips. Returning to the group, Shannon gives Chloe the chips to distribute. Shannon meets with the hostess to pay the tab for everyone's brunch.

******

Chloe returns with their complimentary chips and tells the group, "Okay, folks. Here are your chips and I want to let you know, I will be taking complimentary photos down at the Gator Cove Waterfall, beyond the glass door. I'll have them ready to mail to you on Monday afternoon. So, if anyone wants a photo of their trip here, please meet me down there."

As the morning wears on, Chloe is busy, and as she finishes up with the last guest, she is exhausted. The guests have enjoyed their time in the casino and the photos taken against the backdrop of the running waterfall, green plants, and colorful flowers. A few of the photos included a small gecko or a dark frog. A few included a Roseate Spoonbill, a Sand hill Crane, and a Whooping Crane. A true memory photo. As she takes the last photo, she packs her camera away, and joins Shannon for a latte.

******

After having breakfast with Steve at The Lamplighter Inn, Montana opens the door to Trish's *Cutz and Curlz*, to have her hair highlighted.

Trish smiles, "Well, hi, Montana, how is everything going today? I heard about you and your sisters finding Brent yesterday morning. Why didn't you say something last night?"

"Hi, Trish. I guess I didn't really have anything to say. It's still under investigation, so I can't say anything. But it was devastating for Chloe and

Shannon. They went to school with him. Didn't you, too?"

"Well, I did for about ten years. My Dad moved us here when he lost his job back in Colorado, so I only attended here since second grade. Mom and Dad were from here and knew your family and Wayne's. Wayne's Dad ran the newspaper and Wayne's Mom was the librarian. His Dad pulled in a favor and helped my Dad get hired at the Piper aeronautics plant. My grandparents were glad we moved here. They had wanted us to, for a while. As you know, Mom taught at the school and we stayed with Gram and Gramps until the end of the year. Then we moved into our house on Rose Lane."

"So you did know him?" Montana asked.

"Yeah, I did, not as well as some, though. I ran with another crowd. While Brent was the treasurer of our class, Chloe was the homecoming queen, yours truly, starred in the school play."

Montana laughs along with Trish. "We all have those memories. While my sister, Chloe, was working on being homecoming queen, she was also a cheerleader for four years. She worked on the school yearbook staff, even back then she wanted to be a photographer. And Shannon, played the violin and worked on the school newspaper. That's where she hooked up with Wayne. Of course, by the time I got there, I knew I wanted to be a cop and was a member of the Teens Against Crime Book Club and an avid 4H'er. I was also into horses then, too."

Smiling, Trish says, "I am just about finished here, so you can get out and solve this crime."

******

As Montana leaves the beauty shop and steps out into the sunshine, a soft breeze blows the leaves on the trees. Walking down the street, passing the park, she sees the sparkling fountain in front of the court house. Suddenly thirsty, and thinking a latte would sure hit the spot, and if Mary is here, well, going over Thursday night couldn't hurt. She opens the door of the Artistic License Coffee Shop and enters into the cozy cafe.

The Columbian and Brazilian coffee beans stimulate her senses, and breathing deeply of coffee, vanilla, cocoa, and hazelnut, she walks up to the counter and smiles at Mary. "Hi, Mary, I would like a caramel latte, hold the topping."

"Hi, Montana! It's coming right up. Are you going to take it with you, or are you staying here?"

"Well, I would like to chat with you, if you have a few minutes. When is your break?"

"Not for about fifteen minutes. But I will mix your latte and you can take it to a booth at the window and I will join you there."

"Okay! It sounds good to me." Waiting for Mary to prepare her latte, Montana pays and goes to the booth.

Wondering how the bus tour was going, she was sure the group were having a great time. Bet they had a lot of questions this morning! Sometimes Montana went with her sisters, she liked to play the slots and brunch was always a good spread, but they were meeting Keith and Beth Stewart at the Second Chance Ranch this afternoon and it was much more important to be there. She sighed and sipped her latte.

Mary came over and sat down across from Montana, "Okay, what did you want to talk to me about, Montana?"

"I just wanted to review with you what happened Thursday night. Can we go over it again?"

"Sure, I don't think I have anything to add, though. As I told you Thursday night, Brent came in the shop about 8:15 or 8:30 alone. A man was here in a corner booth. He stood up and Brent went over to him and sat down. I think they shook hands. They talked for a few minutes, I went over to ask if he wanted anything, his companion had ordered a dark roasted blend. Brent shook his head, it seems that he had expected to meet up with this guy."

"Okay, you said Brent went right over to him? Didn't he say a word to you? Not even a hello?"

"That's right, not a word. It didn't matter to me, though. That's the time we usually pickup, so I don't want to chat then, either. I left them alone, and went back to the counter. Max was here too. He was working one side of the room, and I was working the other side, the way we usually do."

"Mary, I have another question for you. Did you notice a briefcase attached to Brent's wrist with a chain."

"No, Brent had his briefcase next to him and his hand was in his lap." Montana paused, sipping her latte, asks Mary, "Can you describe Brent's companion?"

"He was slender and tall, and when he ordered his coffee, he had an Italian accent. I had studied European languages in college. He was wearing Italian leather shoes and Italian cut trousers and jacket. They were dark, I would say black, but it is dark in here, so it could have been any dark shade. He had dark hair and dark eyes and he wore a gold ring."

Surprised, Montana asks, "A gold ring. Did you notice anything else? Anything memorable about the guy or about Brent?"

Mary looks at the clock above the counter and looks back to Montana and says, "No, nothing else. As I said earlier, it was dark in here, you know," she made air quotes "our atmosphere, a gold band, but nothing else. They weren't here long, as I told you Thursday night. They left shortly after Brent came in, now, I better get back to the counter. I work until 3:00 and I am off tomorrow, so I am going to get groceries and get home early. There's a comedy tonight I want to watch on Turner Classics. So I plan on making popcorn, curling up on my couch and snuggle with my cat, Patches."

Montana smiles, "It sounds like a great plan, Mary. I appreciate your telling me again, Mary. Have a good night and I'll see you on Monday. Take care and thanks again."

Going over the conversation in her mind, she finishes her latte and leaves to meet Steve.

******

Later Saturday morning, Montana opens the envelope and takes the photos out and places them on the table. Getting a glass from the cabinet above the sink and filling it with ice, she pours ice tea into her glass. Sitting at the table, she spreads out the photos and looks them over. Her eyes stop on the image of the broken chain and the gold ring.

Hearing the door open, she glances up and smiles at Steve. "Hi, babe."

"Hi, babe. I am looking at the photos Chloe took. Come here and check this out!"

Kissing the top of her fragrant hair he says, "Photos. When did Chloe take those photos?"

As he glances over her shoulder, Montana hurriedly replies, "Look here, at this one." She points out to Steve, "Here is that broken chain, and lying next to Brent, is a gold ring."

Steve replies, "That's a fraternity ring. Ralph's brother, Darrell, has one, too. That is probably Brent's ring lying there."

"No, Steve, Brent's ring was still on his hand when Chloe turned him over. This may have been left by the killer." Glancing from the photo to Steve she adds, "What did the crime scene photos show?"

As they look at each other, Steve shakes his head and says, "When I got to the scene, the bracelet and the ring were not beside the body. "Then he asks, "What did Mary tell you?" Steve pours a glass of ice tea and sits down across from Montana.

"She stayed pretty close to her story from Thursday."

Steve, taking a long drink of tea tells her, "Tell me exactly what she said to you."

"She said Brent came into the coffee shop around 8:30 p.m. A man was seated at a corner booth. He stood up and Brent walked over to him. They both sat down. Mary went over to see if Brent wanted anything, she said he only shook his head no. It seems Brent expected to meet up with this guy."

Steve asks her, "Did she mention the briefcase?"

Montana answered, "Yes, but she said when Brent sat down, he put the briefcase next to him, his hand was concealed beneath the table. He sat on the left side of the booth."

Wondering out loud, Steve says, "So at that time, the security chain was still attached. I did not see the chain or the ring when I arrived at the scene. Did she say anything else about the appearance of the man he met?"

Montana takes another drink of her ice tea and nodding, says, "He had an accent. She had studied languages in college, she recognized it as an Italian accent. Mary did say she saw a gold ring on his hand. She couldn't tell what kind of ring, but she saw it had a gold band."

Surprised, Steve asks, "A gold ring, that's interesting, don't you think?"

Montana nods her head, "Yes it is! You know after looking at this ring, Wayne has one, too. Perhaps he can explain them."

Steve says, "Well, I guess we better get over to Keith's."

They both stand up.

Montana takes the photos and puts them back in the manila envelope and hands them to Steve. "Here Steve, take these. You may want to look at them again."

Steve takes the envelope, goes into his home office, and places them in a drawer in his desk. After securing the house, they climb into Steve's white two- door Ford Ranger pick-up, and head to The Second Chance Ranch.

******

Steve and Montana sit down at the dining room table at the Stewart's. Keith pours ice tea in tall, frosted, ice- filled glasses and places them on a tray to take to the dining room with a dish of lemons. Montana moves the fresh floral arrangement to the right as Beth places a soup tureen full of lobster bisque in the center of the table. Beth returns to the kitchen and brings a tray with warm homemade bread and a bowl of fresh, crisp salad to the table. After sitting and bowing their heads, Keith offers the blessing.

After a few moments, Keith announces, "I spoke to Tennessee this morning, he and Chloe are donating two older mares to Second Chance Ranch for the kids.

Montana, filling a glass plate of salad says, "That's wonderful! I know those mares are docile and easy going and will be perfect for inexperienced hands."

Steve looking over at Montana and wiping his mouth with his napkin, asks, "We're here to help, too. What can we do?"

Beth and Keith look at each other and exchange smiles and, at Beth's nod, Keith says, "Glad you asked. Would you two like to be counselors and riding instructors?"

Steve, taking a spoonful of the delicious soup, says, "Counseling I can do, and I would love to be a part of this camp session. But riding instructor?"

Montana, laughing, says, "You can do both, Steve. As for me I *want* to do both. It sounds like a great time."

The two couples talk about the plans for the coming session. Later, having finished their soup and salad, Beth stands to clear the table and Montana offers to pour coffee.

Beth tells them, "Now that you two have agreed to help with this session, I'll get dessert. I made Key Lime Pie! Let's have the pie and coffee out on the deck, while we visit."

******

While the group is enjoying the slots, roulette table and computer poker, Shannon and Chloe take a much needed break. Taking their iced coffee lattes to the patio, they sit down at a wrought iron table, overlooking the turquoise and gold cove, they enjoy the soothing, relaxing sound of the water fall. Easing their toes out of their shoes, they stretch their slender, tanned legs and wriggle the tension from their legs to their toes.

"Ah, that feels sooo good," Chloe sighs.

Taking a sip of her vanilla latte, Shannon smiles and says, "This is the life! This is sooo good." Offering her glass to Chloe, "Wanna sip?"

Chloe taking Shannon's glass, offers hers in return, "Yum! Try this, it's sooo chocolatey!"

Shannon agrees, "They are both great." Reaching in her bag and removing her planner, Shannon opens it and asks, "Are you ready for the details of our next tour?"

Retrieving her planner from her bag, Chloe nods at Shannon and says, "Shoot!"

"I have narrowed it to two choices: St, Augustine and Jacksonville. Both are week-end packages."

"Well, since this will be the last one this season, I think we need to make it St. Augustine! It's romantic, great food, and I love to take pictures of the fort. There's also shopping, carriage rides, antiques..,"

Laughing, Shannon says, "Whoa sis, you don't have to sell me. St. Augustine it will be. I'll notify our clients so I can start taking reservations." As they finish their lattes, Shannon asks, "About those photos you took yesterday, did you contact Montana?"

Nodding, Chloe says, "Yes, I did. I haven't heard from her yet"

"We'll try to get in touch with her when we get back to Whispering Key. Did you make an extra set?"

"Yes, I have one and I gave her one set. I still have the negatives. Why?"

"I would like to look at them, too. If I can?"

Shrugging her slender shoulders, Chloe says, "I'll give you the set I have in my car when we get back to Whispering Key. I can make another copy tonight when I get home."

"Thanks, Chloe, I appreciate it."

"No problem. I know how you always want to check things out, too." She laughs gently, patting her sister's hand, adding, "I think it's getting to that time. Let's finish up here and go meet the group."

The two girls slip on their shoes and put away their planners. Standing up, they return to the pre-arranged meeting place.

# Chapter Four

The excited guests disembarked the bus back at Trevor Travel Agency. Some had won and others had enjoyed a relaxing afternoon. Shannon takes the bus back to the terminal and returns to the office to finish her paperwork. As Chloe tidies up the kitchenette, the phone rings. Drying her hands on a tea towel, she answers the phone in the kitchenette.

Entering Shannon's office, she says, "Montana's on the phone."

Chloe sits down in the chair across from her sister.

Shannon presses the speaker button and says, "Hey, how's it going, lil sis?"

"Hi, girls, did everyone have fun at the casino?" Chloe sits on the edge of the chair and leans on her elbows and says, "Of course. We had a few winners and everyone enjoyed the super, simple, rich brownies on the return trip. What did you think of my pictures?"

"Steve and I think they're great. Real eye opening, huh?" adding, "Steve was surprised to see the chain and ring in your photos, though, he said they weren't there when he arrived." Montana continues, "Steve also showed me a shadow in the photo, it looks like the image of a person, did you notice it, Chloe?"

Sitting straight in her chair, Chloe says, "No, I didn't!"

Shannon, taking a deep breath asks, "Was there someone in the shadows?"

Quivering, Chloe asks, "Do you mean someone else was there? Someone saw me take those pics?" Slowly standing and beginning to pace, she turns, and looking at Shannon, adds, "I'm scared. Do you think he knows who I am?"

Shannon, walking around the desk, places her arm around her sister, gently hugs her and says, “I think we all need to look out for each other.”

Montana agrees, “Yes, we all have to be careful. Just don't panic.”

“Okay, I'm okay. I'll take another look at the photos, Montana. I have an extra copy here in my car. I'm surprised I didn't see the shadow, but I guess I was so excited to see the chain and ring that I missed the shadow.” Changing the subject, Shannon asks, “How was your visit at the Stewart’s?”

“It went well. We made plans for the week when the kids will be arriving. Where are you guys going to dinner tonight?”

Shannon replies, “I'll have to call Wayne, but I think probably Roger's BBQ. Would you all like to join us? Oh, by the way, Montana, our next trip will be to St. Augustine. Do you think you and Steve might want to join us? It will be our last bus tour this season.”

Chloe excitedly tells them, “I received a call this afternoon from Amy Harris. That weekend, at St Augustine, she is having a show of her new fall line. She asked me to do a photo shoot.”

Montana says, “I'll tell Steve to call Patrick Regan to cover for him. You know I love St. Augustine.”

Chloe says, “I'll call Tennessee and you call Wayne and we'll tell them to meet us at Roger's. We can have a glass of white zin while we wait.”

Montana says, “That sounds good to me. We'll meet you guys there. Bye for now.”

Chloe and Shannon together say, “Bye, Montana.”

The girls quickly call their husbands to let them know dinner's at Rogers. Chloe straightens up the sitting room and wipes off the counter in the kitchenette. Taking the garbage out, Shannon returns and turns out the lights. Chloe and Shannon leave together, locking the door, they climb into their cars and head for Roger's.

Arriving there, Shannon asks Roger for a table for six in the Pit Room instead of the busy dining room.

“Follow me ladies.” Roger says, and seats them at a round wooden table in front of the fireplace.

“Not too many in here tonight, huh, Roger?” Chloe asks, looking around.

“No, just that gentlemen in the corner, he wanted a quiet place, too. I guess he's waiting for someone. Can I get either one of you something to drink?"

"Yes," Chloe sighs, "we both would like a glass of white zin. Thanks."

Roger leaves to get their drink order.

Shannon relaxes in her chair and says, "This is so much nicer than the busy dining room."

Roger returns with their drinks followed by Tennessee and Wayne. Putting the white zin in front of the girls, he places an ice tea in front of Tennessee and a Windsor and water in front of Wayne.

Placing the menus in front of each, he says, "I'll be back to take your meal order shortly."

As he leaves, Montana and Steve arrive, and joining them.

Steve orders, "A white zin for the lady, and a lite beer for me."

Roger nods his head as he leaves and Steve and Montana sit down.

"How was the tour, girls? Win any money?" Tennessee asks sipping his ice tea.

Chloe and Shannon smile and Chloe says, squeezing his hand, "No, love. I didn't play, so our ranch is still safe."

"It went well after we left this morning. They were asking questions about yesterday. I told them it was under investigation and we couldn't discuss it," Shannon says.

"There are a lot of folks asking questions, Shannon," Steve says, taking a drink of his lite beer.

"I dropped the pictures at Montana's this morning," Chloe says.

"Montana, tell them what you discovered."

"Tennessee and Wayne, Chloe's photos show a gold and black signet ring and the chain from the briefcase. Neither of the items were there when Steve arrived."

Tennessee quickly interrupts, "What do you mean they weren't there, Steve?"

Steve warns, "In my crime scene photos, they weren't there. Some unknown person was there at the scene. He saw Chloe snap those pics. Everyone needs to be careful."

Roger interrupts and takes their food orders.

Roger leaves and Tennessee asks, "A ring? What is the description of it?"

"A fraternity ring. I think it's from your fraternity, Wayne. Didn't you belong to the same one as Brent Mathews?" Chloe asks.

"Yes, I did. There were ten of us that year." Wayne says. Removing his ring, he points out his initials WT. Then continuing, "These rings were chosen by my college fraternity at Florida State. We each had our initials engraved inside the band."

Passing the ring around, each one looks at it, and Chloe asks, "There is a date here, too. What does it represent?"

Roger brings their meal orders and everyone is quiet for a few minutes.

Then Wayne says, "That's the date I was accepted into the fraternity. It is the same one in each of our rings."

Passing the ring back to Wayne, Tennessee says, "Get a list of members and you'll have a list of suspects."

Steve says, looking around the table, "We examined Brent's ring and it is the same except for his initials. I know Brent and Darrell have the same ring, Wayne. I take it you were all a part of that fraternity?"

"Yes, "He nods. "We all joined the same year. Off hand, I can only remember Brent Mathews, Charlie Moore, Preston Reynolds, Darrell Andrews and myself. The other five, I'll have to call the fraternity for that information. Would Monday be okay?"

Steve says, "That would be great. At least I would have a starting point. Right now, I have nothing."

Chloe hears her cell phone beep alerting her to a new text message. Reaching in her bag, she reads the message. Dropping the phone to the table, covering her face with her hands, she sobs, "*No!*"

Tennessee wraps his arms around her and picking up the phone, reads the message. He looks around the table, and says through clenched teeth, "He *knows* Chloe took those pics."

Swallowing a bite of ribs, Steve reaches for the phone and says, "This guy means business. We have to get this out in the open."

Wayne, nodding, agrees with Steve and says, "I'll head over to get this in tonight, it will be in tomorrow's early edition."

Shannon, looking at Wayne and over at Chloe, picks up her glass and, after taking a sip says, "Could this draw more attention to Chloe?"

"Someone already knows she took the photos, Shannon," Wayne tells her.

"I wrote down the number of the phone that just texted her. But I imagine it's a pay as you go kind. It may be hard to locate," Montana tells them. "Well, at least we can start there. Here, Chloe. Let us know if you get anything else."

Nodding, Chloe leans against Tennessee.

Stroking her arm, Tennessee says, "I think it's time to get you home." He stands up and throws some cash on the table, "This should be our share, gang. Come on, Chloe. We'll see you all at the service. Okay? Good night."

******

The Saturday night was ablaze with stars and the full moon hung above like a giant spotlight. Wayne and Shannon Trevor leave together from Roger's BBQ . Wayne walks Shannon to her cream Beetle and waits while she unlocks the door.

Turning toward him, Shannon smiles and stands on tiptoe to kiss him goodbye. "You be careful, Shannon. That text message was a surprise and I know this fool isn't done here. You are going straight home, right?"

"No, Wayne. I have to go back to the agency to finish up my paperwork. I don't want to worry about forgetting something by Monday. That text message was a surprise," shaking her dark curls, "but not totally unexpected. Those photos may help identify that man and, well, fear can bring out the worst in us, you know?"

Holding her close to him, he didn't notice a figure standing in the shadows on the side of the building. "You're right, but you found Brent, and , well, just be careful. Okay?"

Giving him a final hug, Shannon smiles up at him, and climbs into her Beetle. Rolling down her window, she tells him, "You don't plan on putting her name in the article, right?"

Bending down to speak to her through her window, he nods and says, "I don't think it will matter, whoever texted her knows already. I just want to stir the pot."

"You're right, honey. I'll be careful. You, too. I'll see you at home later, okay?"

Standing up, Wayne runs his fingers through his hair and says, "It will be much later than you, I'm sure. But I'll get home as soon as I can, okay?"

"Okay."

Putting her car in gear she pulls away from him and takes the road back to her agency.

Wayne takes out his keys and returns to his Charger, climbs in, then drives down to the newspaper office. Thinking this will be a long night, again. He sure hoped she was going to be okay. That text Chloe got during dinner, that was scary. As Wayne pulls into his parking place in front of the Trevor Times, he notices lights are on and Mike Phillips is working.

Wayne thinks... Oh, yeah, he's probably finishing up his special report. "Hey, Mike, you been here long?"

"No, Wayne, I had a late supper down at the Lamplighter and I just got in about a half an hour ago. I plan on being here late, though. What's up? You usually don't come in on a Saturday night."

"Well, I have to get an article out in the first edition. On this murder investigation."

"Okay, I'll keep to myself. I have your interview and I also interviewed a few friends of Brent's."

"Oh really? Who?"

"While I was down having supper, I ran into three of them, Charlie Moore, Preston Reynolds and Marcus Magliano. They were discussing Brent, so I asked if I could interview them." Picking up his notes, he shows them to Wayne. "What do you think?"

Wayne reads and says, "This is really good, Mike. Are you planning on putting this in the morning edition?"

"Yep, that's why I'm here, boss." He smiles and adds, "Thanks."

"Well, let's get this out. I'll type my article and you can finish up there and then we both can get home early."

The two reporters get to work. Later as they get ready to leave, Wayne asks Mike, "Who are the next folks you plan on interviewing?"

"Well, I want to meet with David Thomas and I'd like to interview Shannon. Do you think she'd agree to an interview?"

"I'll see what she says, Mike. Did you make an appointment with David?"

"I called this evening and set up one for Monday morning. I will be interviewing Brent's folks on Monday, too."

"Well, that sounds great. If you need any help, let me know."

"Will do, boss."

The two men head home.

******

In the cozy cabin, at Castlekeep Ridge, Montana and Steve are sharing a brownie sundae and watching TV.

"These brownies are delicious," Steve tells her, as he takes the last creamy bite of brownie, nuts, and whipped cream.

"Yeah, they are. Chloe packed a few for us from this afternoon bus trip."

"The bus trip?" Nodding his head, he smiles, "Oh, yeah, the famous 'dessert bus extraordinaire'." He laughs.

Finishing up her dessert, she stands and gestures for his dessert bowl. "You better get hold of Patrick, Steve. Our trip is scheduled in a few weeks."

"Yeah, babe, I know, I know. I'll do that now." He turns the volume down on the crime drama they were watching and pulls out his cell from the pocket of his jeans. "Patrick, this is Steve Blake. I just wanted to see if you had a chance to make those arrangements for my vacation?"

"Well, I tentatively put in for the time. I just have to let them know exactly a week or so ahead of time. I'm not tied up with anything that I can't get away from here. Just a couple of long term crimes I'm working on. A lot of that I can continue with there at Whispering Key."

"Well if it's okay with you our trip to St. Augustine is scheduled for the first of May."

"Isn't that the start of the sailboat races, too?"

"I guess it is." Laughing, "Do you think you'd like to take a chance at beating me?"

"Oh, I will, my friend, because I'll have that weekend you're gone to practice."

"Okay, sounds like a bet my friend. I'll try not to beat you too bad." Sharing another laugh, Steve says, "Better go, I've got an investigation here that I'll want to tie up. So I'll be in great need of a relaxing weekend. Thanks, buddy."

"Looking forward to the time away, too, my friend. Talk to you later." Patrick hangs up.

Montana, sitting down next to him, smiles and says, "All set?"

"All set, babe, for our weekend get-away." He scoots back on the couch and she snuggles next to him and taking the remote control, turns up the volume of their drama.

******

Saturday night at Quantico, Virginia, Patrick stretches and hangs up the phone. Returning to the kitchen for another cup of coffee, he smiles at Steve's bet. They sure enjoyed teasing each other.

All around him were mementos of his life with Sarah and Lily. Snapshots of time and tender moments between his family of three. Sarah's mystery books and gardening tools, Lily's story books, a cup of clay she did in day care and a framed picture of seashells she made when they returned from visiting Steve Blake at Whispering Key that last summer they were together.

Life was good, Sarah had fought and won her battle with breast cancer and they celebrated with that trip to Steve's. They had talked about having a sibling for Lily. They both were only children and they wanted Lily to have a brother or sister. Then, at her check-up, the tests showed cancer was back in her body. This time there was no cure. Just time, precious time for the three of them.

One day, Lily was out playing and she saw a kitten in the road, running out to save it from an oncoming car, she was killed. The sound of metal meeting flesh still haunted him, and the sound of grief and pain from Sarah as she ran out to reach her baby. A neighbor called 911, but, when the ambulance arrived, it was too late. She had died in her parents arms, still holding the tiny kitten. Chills suddenly went through him and goose bumps beaded on his arms. Sarah hadn't lasted too long after that fateful day.

Standing up, he returns his cup to the kitchen and picks up a picture of a happier moment. Sarah and Lily dressed for a tea party, floppy hats and pretty dresses. Lily had not talked of anything else for days afterwards. Replacing the photo in its place of honor on the white desk in the kitchen, he calls his yellow lab Molly and they take a walk. Thinking, yes, this will be good for Molly and him, this trip. Maybe it's time he moved on...

******

Shannon pulls into her parking place and looks around her as she exits the vehicle. Holding her keys in her hand, she approaches the door and enters the agency. Locking the door behind her, she turns on the lights and enters the office. Removing her bag from her shoulder, she lowers it into the bottom drawer of her Queen Anne, oak, writing desk. Then, pulling the folder toward her, she finishes up the paperwork. About an hour and a half later, she stands up and places the folder into her filing cabinet and pulls her hobo bag from the bottom drawer. After leaving her office, she turns off the lights as she exits.

Stepping outside , she breathes deeply of the evening breeze and looks warmly across the street to the art museum, all lit up by security lights. Soon, she will be back working over there, repairing paintings, and helping David care for the art relics and sculptures. There may be new additions, but there are always the old ones needing continuing care. Leaving the shelter of the doorway, Shannon walks quickly to her Beetle, unlocks the door, and climbs into the car, and starts it up. To home, a cup of relaxing tea, a bath, then bed. She was so tired…

Pulling out of the parking place, she drives slowly down the street and turns to her neighborhood, not noticing that a late- model, dark car was following her as she left the agency. Unexpectedly, she feels a car hitting her from behind. Suddenly, Shannon is hit again, and looking through the rearview mirror, she sees the car is too close for identification. It appears to be on her bumper. Quickly she accelerates the motor and speeds away, but the car is following close behind her. She takes a quick, right turn away from her neighborhood and heads out on the highway, thinking, maybe Montana can shed some light on this.

The car stays on her bumper, and after a few minutes, falls back. Trying to get a better view of the pursuing car, she thinks maybe she's mistaken. She speeds up and begins the climb up the ridge to Montana's cabin. The lights are on and she is glad to see they are still awake. Suddenly, the car behind her bumps her hard and she grabs onto the steering wheel as she realizes she may not make it. Trying to gain control again, she turns a hard right to the last exit before the climb. Turning sharply, she bounces on the dirt and comes to a stop in the trees up ahead, hitting her head on the steering wheel as she stops. A few minutes later she opens her eyes and realizes she is alone.

Unfastening her seat belt, she reaches for her cell phone and realizes it has fallen on the floor along with her purse, its contents scattered everywhere. Opening her door, she climbs out of the Beetle, trembling as she stands up, she leans back against the car and pushes her curls away from her face, gingerly touching the lump forming on her forehead. Turning, she notices she has a flat tire, too! Sliding down the door of her car, she lands on the soft leaves and dirt, and pulling her legs up to her chest, she places her head on her knees. Suddenly, it became too much for her, she cries tears of fear, disappointment and shock.

After a few minutes, it seemed longer, she glances up through the trees above her head at the star- filled, velvet sky. The breeze blows gently on her face and dries her tears. Looking up the road toward the cabin, she sees the lights are off and Steve and Montana are probably in bed. Not knowing the time, she cautiously stands up, opens the door, and retrieves her cell from the floor. Gathering up the contents in her bag, she remembers the tape and the key. Frantically running her hand in the bag, she locates both.

Dialing 911, she waits to be connected. Shannon tells the operator her situation and hangs up the phone. Glancing down at the phone, she sees the time is later than she imagined. But then after all, Steve and Montana were asleep. Oh, Wayne! Quickly dialing the phone, she reaches Wayne and tells him the news. Wayne wants to come get her, but she assures him help is on the way. In the distance, she hears the sirens and watches as the squad car pulls into the clearing beside her. Mike O'Rourke steps out of the squad car and walks up to her.

"I-I know I hit my head on the steering wheel and I have a flat tire, too. But I think I'll skip the hospital and go home, could someone take me home?"

"Sure, Shannon, I will. Your car can be towed. You and Wayne can discuss with the insurance company the repairs needed. If you bumped your head, you shouldn't drive for a couple days."

"Thanks, Mike, I appreciate the ride."

"Uh, did you get lost, or how did you get here?"

"No, I didn't get lost. I was followed and the other car ran me off the main road. I took the exit to escape him."

"Him, did you recognize him?"

"No, I didn't, Mike. The lights from the car blinded me. I think it was a late model, though."

"Well, let's get you out of here and home. Does Wayne know? Is he aware of what happened?"

"Yes, he knows. You know, suddenly, I am so tired."

"Here, let me help you to the squad car. "Then, turning to the tow truck driver, he motions to the Beetle, and tells him, "Lee, take this over to your place and wait for a call from Wayne. He'll have to get hold of his insurance agent."

"Okay, Officer Mike, will do."

As the tow truck driver goes to finish his job, Mike O'Rourke turns to Shannon and carries her to his squad car. Within a few minutes, he arrives at the Trevor's home, all lit up. Watching for the car, Wayne quickly runs out and opens the door and lifts up his wife tenderly in his arms.

"Thanks, Mike, I appreciate this. I wanted to go get her, but she told me to wait here. I have been pacing all night wondering about her and where she's at."

"Well, she's here now, and the Beetle is towed over at Lee's. You can contact him tomorrow after you talk to your insurance agent."

"What happened, Mike?"

"She said she was being followed, too close for her to identify the other driver. She tried to avoid him by taking the exit toward Castlekeep Ridge. I think she had been out for a while before she called for assistance. When did she call you?"

"Out for a while? She must have called me right after she called 911. I probably should get her some medical care. If she'll let me."

"Well, good luck on that one, Wayne. I know how these girls are. Stubborn! So I suggest giving her an aspirin and apply ice to that lump. Keep an eye on her, don't want a concussion."

Wayne nods his head and asks, "Did she recognize the driver or the car?"

"No, she says she didn't. She said that the driver stayed too close for her to have a chance to see. The driver kept his lights in her mirror, so she was blinded by the lights, too. She took the exit to Castlekeep Ridge probably from memory. Shannon had a flat tire and there may be more damage on the Beetle. I'm sure Lee's Towing will let the agent back there to check it out, and of course, we'll have to check, too. It may not be ready for a few days, before the repairs can be done."

Wayne nods his head and turns to go back inside. Mike O'Rourke climbs back in the squad car and heads back to the station. Wayne kicks the door closed with his foot and climbs the stairs to their bedroom. Gently laying her on the bed , she rouses, and he removes her shoes and covers her with an extra blanket.

She looks up at him and he strokes her face, and asks, "Do you want me to take you to the hospital? I'm worried about you, sweet pea."

Shaking her head she tells him, "No,.. so tired. Just an aspirin and an ice bag. I'll...be fine."

She falls back to sleep and then stirs again, when he returns with the aspirin and water, then he runs down to the kitchen to get a bag of ice Running back upstairs he places the ice bag on her head and pulls up the blanket and descends the stairs.

Mixing a Windsor and water, he sits down on the couch and picks up the phone to call Steve. "Hey, Steve, this is Wayne Trevor."

"Uh… hi, Wayne. It's late, is everything okay?"

"No, it's not. Shannon was followed tonight and had some trouble, actually out near your place. I'm really concerned about all this. First this texting with Chloe and now Shannon."

Running his fingers through his hair, Steve suddenly sits upright, and Montana wakes to hear him ask, "Shannon, what happened? Is she okay?"

"No, she was run off the road. Officer O'Rourke brought her home and the tow truck towed the car. I'll call the insurance agent tomorrow morning. She hit her head but she refused to seek medical care. Right now, I'm just keeping an eye on her. She refused to go to the hospital, even with me."

"Well, I'm going to call Mike, Wayne. Did she recognize the car or the driver?"

"No, she didn't. Mike said she was blinded by the headlights, and, well the driver stayed too close to allow space for her to identify the car."

"Well, that sounds like he knew what he was doing. I think this guy means business. But I don't understand what Shannon might have known, that would be a reason for this. Now Chloe well, she took those photos, and that kind of tagged her for trouble. I'll see what I can find out."

"I know you will Steve, thanks. I'll talk to you tomorrow at church. That's if Shannon is up to it."

"Right man, good night." Wayne hangs up the phone, sits back and wonders, what's going on?

******

"Well, well, well! They have in evidence a picture of a broken security chain and a ring. How are you going to change this unwanted info?"

"Just calm down. There is no way for them to tie it to me. No one knows I'm here."

"Well, what about the pictures? You need to get them and be sure what's there."

"I watched Chloe take those pictures, she probably has the negatives at her studio. I'll get them, check them out, and burn them."

"What about what the cops have?"

"I'll take care of those, too!

******

Montana, pulling herself up in the bed, pulls the covers down in her lap and asks, "What was that about? Did something happen to Shannon?"

Turning to her, he nods and says, "Yeah, babe. She was run off the road tonight. I thought she was on her way home after dinner at the BBQ place. But, I guess she didn't go straight home."

Her hazel eyes looked deep into his, and says, "I take it she didn't recognize the driver or the car?"

"No, she didn't. Wayne said it was near here. She must have decided to come here and see us about something, Montana."

Pulling her tousled hair back from her face, she shakes her head and says, "No, she didn't say anything to me. I guess we'll have to wait to talk to her tomorrow. Wayne take her to the hospital?"

Smiling at her, he says, “You know how stubborn you girls are. Wayne tried, but she wouldn't budge. He said they'd see us tomorrow at church. That is unless Shannon decides not to. She was pretty shaken up and she hit her head pretty hard. So she may have a lump the size of a baseball, or at least a bruise.” Steve adds, “I'm going to call Mike, real quick, babe, okay?”

“Sure go ahead.”

Quickly, Steve dials the station and on the pick- up asks, “Hey, Mike. I just got the word from Wayne about Shannon. Is there anything he might not have known? Have you discovered anything else?”

“Uh, no, Chief, I don't have anything to add yet. Just what Shannon told me when I got there. I take it she didn't go to the hospital?”

“No, she didn't, Mike. Well, write up what you got and I'll stop by in the morning to check the report. If you discover anything between now and then, call, okay? We've got to figure this out.”

“Sure will, Chief.” Steve places the phone in the cradle and turns toward Montana. “He didn't have anything else to add. So, I guess we'll have to wait for tomorrow.”

“Yeah, babe. It will be here before you know it. But I don't think we'll see them tomorrow, at least, not at church. But we can call them or stop by after the service. I'm going to want to hear it from her myself. Maybe she'll give me more information. Right now, it's probably all still a shock and a blur.”

Then, opening her arms to her lover, he lays down beside her. Together they lay awake until the Sunday morning dawn streaks the sky. And the phone rings....

Groggily, Steve answers, “Yeah, Blake here.”

“Steve, this is Ron Stevens from the AAA Alarm Co., we have a break-in at Chloe's Moments Studio."

## Chapter Five

"Mrs. Hope, this is Ron at the AAA Alarm Co. We had an alarm at the studio and I have notified the police."

"Thanks, Ron, I'm on my way there, now." Chloe places the phone back on the charging cradle, setting on the night stand beside her side of the bed. Tennessee is crawling out from under the covers and walks over to the closet.

By the time Chloe has gotten up and peeled off her navy, silk camisole and matching pajama bottoms, slipping into jeans and pulling a pink tee over her head, Tennessee has slid into jeans and pulling his navy blue tee shirt over his head he says, "I'll drive. I know you are upset, not knowing what might be damaged."

Startled, she moves toward Tennessee, "This is what I was afraid of."

They jump into Tennessee's burgundy and black jeep Wrangler. As he pulls to a stop light, Chloe glances at the corner and reads the headlines on the newspaper inside the vending box.

"Quick, stop, give me 75 cents for a paper."

"Chloe, have you lost your mind? We get the paper, at the ranch."

"I know, but I have to see it *now*!"

Tennessee pulls over to the curb, hands Chloe three quarters, and puts the Jeep in park. Chloe jumps out, gets the paper, and reads quickly through the article.

She tells Tennessee, "It doesn't say who took the photos, but *he* knows it was me and the murderer must have thought I would develop them at my studio. Most people don't know I have a darkroom at home. Oh, Tennessee, what if he breaks into our house, he might, as he wouldn't have found anything he was looking for at the studio."

"You're right, I'll call Steve, then we'll get to the studio to see what is what."

"Steve, this is Tennessee, we're on our way to the studio...oh, you're already there? Could you dispatch a cruiser to Hope Ranch, Chloe is afraid that the guy might hit our house, too. Yeah,...We'll be there in two minutes."

When Tennessee pulls the Jeep into the parking lot alongside the white building, he and Chloe jump out. In the early morning light of the sunrise, the flashing lights of three squad cars light the parking lot. Chloe and Tennessee head for the rear entrance. The door is standing open, and as Chloe and Tennessee pass through the doorway, they see the splintered wood where the door was forced open. The door leads to a small foyer and the door to the darkroom is standing open.

As they enter the darkroom, Chloe 's heart drops, as she and Tennessee see all the file cabinets have been ransacked and all the negatives and files are scattered all over the floor. Pieces of equipment have been thrown from the work table.

They carefully walk out of the darkroom, and proceed to the front of the building. The middle room, the room she uses for indoor portraits, seemed to be undisturbed. The very expensive lights on poles and her backdrops were in the very same place she had left them.

The front room, or sitting room, was set up like a cozy living room. This is where she spoke with her clients, before and after the portraits were taken. As they turned to go back to the darkroom, Chloe stops and slowly turns around. Gazing above the sofa, her eyes soften as she looks at her beloved copy, of the painting, *The Rehearsal on Stage* by Edgar Degas, which was still undisturbed. Sighing at the disturbing scene around her she wipes tears from her face as Tennessee puts his arm around her and together they slowly walk back to where the forensic team is taking pictures and checking for prints.

Walking through the backdoor to the parking lot, they find Steve leaning with his back against his squad car, completing the paper work of his report. Glancing at Tennessee and Chloe, he tells them, "The cruiser I sent to your ranch called me back and everything is clear out there."

Chloe, looking at Steve, says, "Thanks, Steve. I'm so relieved. This," gesturing around her, "is enough to deal with right now."

Tennessee, pacing in front of Steve, tells him, "I can't believe this! The darkroom is ransacked, but that is the only disturbance. First, the text, now this. He knows she has those photos, Steve. I don't think he's going to stop until he gets them."

Steve looks at Tennessee and says, "No, Tennessee. I don't think he will. We've got to get the answers. Maybe these prints will help. "Then adding, "I'll follow you home and check things out one more time."

******

The bells ring out from the white brick bell tower of the Grace Community Church. The sunlight shines through the stained glass windows onto the laminated floor as the organ plays an old hymn. The congregation enters and is seated in the wooden pews.

The service begins and after the worship and sermon, Pastor Keith stands and steps up to the pulpit to make the announcements. "Brothers and sisters, we have some disturbing news on the loss of our Brother, Brent Mathews. He was found dead on Friday morning. Now, I would like Brother Darrell Andrews to give us the details of his visitation and interment."

Darrell stands and comes forward, "Ladies and Gentlemen, Brent Mathews, visitation will be on Tuesday evening from 6:00 till 9:00 p.m. and the memorial service will be here at Grace Community Church on Wednesday at 10:00 a.m. Interment will be at Lighthouse Gardens. Ladies of Grace Society will prepare a lunch to follow, in honor of Mr. Brent Mathews."

He returns to his seat next to his wife, Trish Andrews.

After a brief silence out of respect, Pastor Keith walks back to the pulpit and, smiling, makes an announcement. "Ladies and Gentlemen, I have another announcement on behalf of The Second Chance Ranch. Brother Tennessee and Sister Chloe Hope, please stand. Will Brother Steve Blake and Sister Montana Castle also stand. "The congregation shuffles as the four members stand. "I would like to take this opportunity to thank The Hopes for the donation of two docile and well-mannered standard-bred mares to The Second Chance Ranch." After a brief moment of applause, he continues, "Steve Blake and Montana Castle have agreed to work with Beth and I during our next camp for the kids, teaching horseback riding and the care of the horse." After another moment of applause, he finishes, "We are so blessed to have these folks, and also you brothers and sisters, for your help with this non-profit organization that helps physically and emotionally abused kids from the foster care program. This gives them a chance to 'be kids again and to forget, for a few days, their pain, their disappointments and their disability.' Now, may each of you have a blessed day and thank you for worshipping with us today. Now, let us pray."

******

Wayne and Shannon Trevor are seated at their kitchen table enjoying a light breakfast of fruit and bagels.

Wayne pours a refill of coffee and places Shannon's cup in front of her and says, "Feeling better now that you have something on your stomach?"

"Yes, Wayne, thank you. After this second cup of coffee, I may begin to start feeling somewhat normal."

Smiling, Wayne opens the newspaper on the table and begins reading the headlines

The phone rings, Shannon picks it up and says, "Good morning, Shannon here."

"Oh, Shannon, Steve and I were wondering if we could stop by, that is, if you're up for company."

"Oh, of course, Montana, that would be great. How was service?"

"It was wonderful, Pastor Keith announced our involvement and Chloe's and Tennessee's donation."

"Well, I am glad things are going so well for the coming camp session."

"Uh, yeah, that wasn't all, Shannon, he had Darrell announce Brent's visitation and interment."

Sighing, Shannon says, "Uh, how are his folks doing? Were they there?"

"Yes, they were. Doc said he had talked with Wayne and he had agreed to read the eulogy."

"Yes, he did." Reaching for Wayne's hand across the table, she adds, "I know he is glad they asked."

"Well, Steve and I will be over in a bit. We want to change our clothes. Okay?"

"That would be great. I'll have the coffee on," She hangs up the phone and tells Wayne, "That was Montana and she gave me the update on Brent's visitation and burial. She said she had spoken with Doc and he told her you were doing the eulogy. Oh, they'll be here in a bit."

"Well, I'll clean this up, Shannon. You, my dear, "He tells her, helping her stand up, "need to go upstairs and shower and change. I don't think you'll want to meet your guests, even if it's family, like this."

Laughing softly, Shannon takes his hands and stands up, cautiously, then tells him, "Yes, you're right. It may take me a bit, too. Could you start another pot of coffee?"

"Sure will. Now get on upstairs." He gently pushes her toward the stairwell with a few playful pats.

******

After the service that morning, David Thomas and his wife, Emilee, take their coffee to the sunroom in the back of their Victorian home at 109 Heather Lane in the White Place subdivision a historical landmark of Whispering Key. It had been previously owned by one of the founders of the community, Samuel Anderson. The Thomas had purchased it from the last relative of the founder, when they were married.

Sitting across from each other, David glances up from the Trevor Times and, looking at his petite wife asks, "Well, dear, what do you think of this news about photos discovered. Do you think these photos may help identify the killer?"

"I don't know. But, I bet Shannon will find out who and check it out."

Smiling, David agrees, "Yes, our local reporter/investigator will not let any stone go unturned."

"Not if she can help it. I hope all is okay this morning. I missed them at service. But Montana and Chloe didn't seem too concerned. So maybe it was from a late night."

"Well, later we'll find out when we meet for our dinner at the Walnut Hill Country Club."

"Yes, the reservations are for 4:00 o'clock."

"That's great, honey. I am looking forward to getting together with everyone. What do you make of this relic issue?"

"Well, I'm sure Steve is doing all he can, and there are other relics for the display tonight, right?"

"Oh, yes, my dear. I have spoken to my connection in Rome. I am awaiting a return call." Standing, he takes their two cups and heads for the kitchen, saying, "I'll get refills."

"Thanks, dear. That would be great." She opens the book she is reading, a current mystery of her book club."

Filling their cups with a dark roasted brew, he carries the cups back into the sunroom. Suddenly the phone rings, "I'll get it, Emilee." Picking up the phone, the sound of static can be heard on the line. "Pronto, David, this is Claude. I am returning your call. I have been notified by your police department, a Signor Steve Blake. He let me know about the missing relic and the death of our friend, Brent Mathews. Did you know him well?"

"Yes, yes I did, Claude. A great loss. He has worked for me many times during his college days. He is a close friend of Emilee's and mine as well."

"I wanted to reassure you David, that we know you are doing all you can to solve this, and you will keep us informed. We will keep in touch, yes."

"Of course, Claude. Give my regards to Signor D'Amico. It has been a long time since we've chatted."

"Oh, of course. The same with your lovely wife."

"Will do." Hanging up the phone, he returns to the sunroom carrying the two cups carefully, hands one to Emilee, sits down, and takes a sip of his coffee. "I take it that was Claude?"

"Yes, he said he is aware of everything here and gives you his regards."

"He is such a nice man. He has always made me feel welcome in his world." Reaching over and patting his wife's hand, he smiles and says, "You are, my dear. A great asset to the culture of our little town, too."

"As are you, David. That's why I am so excited about this business venture I am beginning. I want to thank you for your support, darling."

"That's what I'm for, my dear." Picking up the newspaper, he sits back and says, "This article says there are pictures. I hope that our friends Chloe and Shannon will not be in any danger."

"I know. I worry about them, too. First, the discovery of the body and now this thing about pics being discovered. I just hope there won't be any trouble."

Picking up his crossword puzzle, he tells her, "I am sure Montana and Steve will stay on top of things."

Nodding, and picking up her book from her lap, she sits back and opens it to a bookmarked page.

******

Steve and Montana arrive at the door of Wayne and Shannon's red brick and white Cape Cod home. Wayne opens the door and leads them to the sitting room. Montana sits down beside Shannon on the blue and yellow plaid couch. Steve follows and sits on the matching chair. Wayne goes into the kitchen and returns with mugs of coffee and a plate of peanut butter blossoms.

"Now, what happened last night?" Montana asks, taking a cookie from the plate.

"Well, I went back to the agency to do some paperwork. I was there no more than an hour and a half."

"So, you were followed from the agency?"

"Yes. I had just turned toward my neighborhood when he bumped me the first time, so I took a detour to try to escape."

"That's why you were heading in our direction?"

Nodding, Shannon's bottom lip trembles and she says, "I know it was a mistake going up that ridge but I thought he wouldn't follow."

"Did you recognize the driver or the car?"

"No, as I told Officer O'Rourke, he stayed close behind me. His lights blinded me."

"Well, now you've had some time to rest on it, can you remember anything that might help in the investigation?" Steve says.

"Well, when I was climbing up the road he fell back a bit and I could see that the car was a dark late- model sedan."

Montana says, "Are you sure?"

"Yes, I'm sure. Why?" Shannon asks.

"That's the same type of car Brent Mathews rented. It was parked in front of the art museum on Thursday night. It was gone when I left the coffee house."

"We knew he had one, but when Mike O'Rourke called the Lamplighter Inn, it wasn't there. As far as I know, that car has not been located." Steve says, standing up.

"The Lamplighter Inn, I was wondering where he was staying. Shannon and I offered him the apartment above her agency. He never came for the key." Wayne says.

I think I better check on that." Steve tells them. Then, looking down at Montana. "Now I think we better get going, Montana. Will you two be joining us at the country club this evening for dinner?"

"Yes, we will. I am going to play a round of golf with Doc Mathews. Shannon will be home here, resting, so we will be able to join you guys."

"Then we'll see you there."

Steve and Montana leave and Wayne gathers the plate of cookies and mugs, returns them to the kitchen and places them in the dishwasher.

"Now, young lady. You better get upstairs and rest. I'll see you about 3:00. I talked to the insurance agent and he is taking care of the repairs. Your Beetle should be available in a day or two. Until then, if you need to drive, please wait until tomorrow. But, I'll leave you my Charger."

"Okay, Wayne. Have a good game. Give him my love, okay? I'm going to call Miss Mary about having lunch this week. Right now, I think they need the extra company."

"Yes, they do. They always treated us like family. So I'm glad we're here for them." Bending down to kiss her, he leaves to get ready for his game.

******

After her nap, Shannon turns the teakettle on and, as she waits for the whistle, leans against the counter thinking about the last few days. Smiling, she thinks that Wayne and Doc were probably having a great time. She knew Doc played well, but Wayne..? She picks up the phone and dials the Mathews home, knowing Miss Mary was probably enjoying the absence of Doc, as time for her to work in her garden. She could just see her with her bright green, floppy straw hat and her white coat on the ground weeding or transplanting the flowers she takes such pride in.

"Hello?"

"Oh, Miss Mary, this is Shannon. I hope I 'm not disturbing you. I know Doc is with Wayne and I thought I'd call and see how you were doing."

"Well, dear, I'm doing okay, considering things. I needed some therapy, so, I'm out here in my garden, relieving my stress."

Shannon could hear the smile in her voice. "I called to invite you for lunch this week. How about Tuesday afternoon?"

"Oh, Shannon, that would be lovely. Tuesday night is the visitation, so, it will be a nice break for me. What time and do you want to come here?"

"Uh, no, you are a great coOkay, but I want to buy you lunch at The Lamplighter Inn, if that's okay with you? Could you meet me there about 1:00 or would you rather I pick you up?"

"No, dear, I'll drive, and I'll meet you there at 1:00. Everything okay with you, dear?"

"Yes, Miss Mary. Wayne and I are both fine. Just concerned about you and Doc."

"Oh, well, thank you, dear. You both have been great. We appreciate you both so much. It's just you know, with Brent, our son,...well, we miss him so much."

Hearing the tears in her voice, Shannon quickly says, "Oh, I know. We'll be here for you two. You two will be okay eventually."

"Oh, I know, dear. You and your sisters have had your share of loss, too."

"Yes, and even when we didn't think we would, our inner strength came and with each day we learned to let go of our folks, still missing them, but the memories we have, well, that lightens the loss a bit. And we know we will all be together again. Right now we enjoy time with each other and with our friends. You guys are so much a part of our family, Miss Mary."

"And so shall we, in time. But I will be looking forward to having lunch together on Tuesday at 1:00. Thank you so much, Shannon. You are the daughter I never had. Tell your sisters hi from me. See you on Tuesday."

"All right, I'll see you then." After hanging up the phone, she thinks, I wonder if Emilee is available to meet for lunch on Monday. Picking up the phone again, she dials Emilee Thomas.

Emilee answers the phone, David had gone to take a shower and get ready for the evening festivities. "Hi, this is Emilee."

"Oh, Emilee, this is Shannon. Am I catching you at a bad time?"

"No, Shannon, not at all." Sitting down on the sage green rocker, she continues. "It's always nice to get a call from you. Is everything okay? I missed you this morning. It was a great service and Pastor Keith gave us the information on Brent Mathews. What do you need?"

"I was wondering if we can have lunch tomorrow at The Mockingbird Nest?"

"Sure, it sounds great. You want me to pick you up? Or meet you there?"

"That would be great, Emilee. Could you pick me up about 11:00?"

"Sure will, I'll see you tonight, right?"

"Oh, yes, Wayne and I are looking forward to getting together."

"Well, good. So are we. I'll see you tonight and again I'll see you at your agency at 11:00, right?"

"Yes, tonight and again for lunch tomorrow. See you later."

Hanging up the phone, Shannon smiles and leans back in her rocking chair. *Tomorrow, I am going to do some amateur detective work.* Picking up her cup of tea, she smiles and thinks, Yes, tomorrow....

******

Chloe and Tennessee are sharing coffee while Tennessee is watching a harness race. Chloe is reading the latest mystery selection from their book club and the two of them are enjoying a beautiful afternoon.

The phone rings and Chloe picks up the phone beside her and answers, "Hi, Montana, how are you and Steve doing?"

"We're fine. We just left Shannon's and Wayne. You know that they weren't in church this morning, so, we stopped by to check out how she's doing."

"Yes, I guess I was just too preoccupied with my own problems. Is everything okay over there?"

"No, she was followed and run off the road last night, actually, near our place. Do you know of any reason why she would be in danger?"

Laying her book face down in her lap, she says, "No, Montana, I don't. Not unless the person who saw me snap those pictures thinks she may know something, too. Although, I do remember now, she asked for the copy of the pictures I had with me in the car. So I gave that copy to her, came home and made one more. Have you asked her?"

"No, she wasn't very forward with any information. She did say the car that ran her off the road, was a late-model, dark color sedan. That was the same type car that was parked in front of the art museum Thursday night. I know it's a rental car. Steve said it hadn't been located."

"Well, that is interesting! Whoever killed Brent could still have that car. That is one loose thread we need to find and cut off before it causes more damage."

"I agree. Steve is down at the rental agency checking to see if it's been returned yet. I'm sure he has already visited the impounding area. Perhaps he can identify the color of the car, she says he hit her Beetle a few times. So maybe he'll find a match on the bumper."

"Well, I'll keep my eye out for a dark late- model sedan. If I see one, I'll make sure you are notified."

"Thanks, Chloe. You two planning on going to the gathering at the country club this afternoon?"

"Yes, we are. I guess I better get off here so I can go and begin my miracle transformation that I need to do. Or I won't make it. Take care and we'll see you guys there."

"Oh, okay. Will see you later."

******

Chloe and Tennessee follow the maitre d' to their table. The maitre d' pulls out the chair for Chloe, and hands her a menu. Tennessee sits down next to her and, taking his menu from the maitre d', greets everyone.

The waiter takes Chloe and Tennessee's drink order and says, "I'll be back with your drinks and take everyone's dinner selections."

After returning with their drinks and taking their orders, conversation resumes among the old friends.

David waits for a lull in the conversation and asks, "Steve, did you hear back from Claude de Pellegrino about the print you were able to lift from the authenticity papers in the briefcase? Any prints from the briefcase?"

Taking a sip of his ice tea, he replies, "Yes, the print lifted is that of the curator, Anthony D'Amico. I take it he's the curator in Rome, so Claude may know him."

Nodding his white head, David wipes his mouth with his linen napkin and says, "Yes, Steve, he is. I know him, too. He's been employed there in Rome as long as I have here." Smiling, he adds, "We went to school together, when I was a young man."

"Well, since it's expected, we have to look closer. Whoever opened the briefcase was very careful and didn't leave any prints. But, the lock, well, that may tell us a different story. As you all can expect, I can't say anything more."

After a few minutes of eating their meals, Tennessee looks around the table and, taking a sip of water, says, "For those who don't know, Chloe's studio was broken into early this morning."

Everyone gasps, and Steve says, "Wayne's article must have alerted the murderer that we are aware of the fact that evidence has been removed. He is trying to undermine our investigation." Looking around the table, he adds, "That's not all he's done. We are currently checking out some additional information that Shannon has given us last night."

Shannon nods and Wayne says, "Shannon was followed last night, and run off the road."

"I'm fine now though, everyone," Shannon quickly says looking around at her friends and family. "Just this little bump on my head. Now, let's change the subject, okay?"

The group continues discussing the upcoming art exhibit and, as they finish and begin to leave, Shannon taps her glass with her spoon, and smiling, tells them, "Friends, our next tour will be to St. Augustine, Florida. You are all invited, it will be a great time for romance and there will be a fashion show that weekend, too. So you can even check out the fall fashions."

Chloe smiles and adds, "You all remember Max 's sister, Amy Harris? She will be previewing her fall line that weekend in St. Augustine. She has asked yours truly to do the publicity photos and the shoot at the show. It's going to be so exciting! I know you all will want to be there to support her."

The party breaks up and Steve pulls Chloe aside and says, "Chloe, I need to have your negatives of the scene. When would be a good time for you?"

"I need to go to the studio, in the morning, I can drop them off at the station."

Shannon suggests, "Why don't I meet you at the studio?"

Before Chloe has a chance to respond, Montana quickly says, "I'll be there too. Tell me what time?"

Chloe looking at her two sisters, smiling, says, "Thank you two. Is 9:00 too early?"

******

Later that Sunday evening at The Shetland Art Museum, David smiles and greets the community coming to view the exhibit. He leads the tour for his friends through the relic exhibit and excitedly explains each one. One exhibit displayed a gold coin circa A.D. 120 on green velvet. The second exhibit showed off a French, cameo, glass footed bowl from the 19$^{th}$ Century surrounded by rose petals. The third relic was a 9-inch Pre-Columbian Character Mask atop a marble pillar. The final exhibit displayed a porcelain sculpture of a lady from the 19$^{th}$ Century France, standing proudly against black velvet. Track lighting above each display cast a smooth glow to each piece and the oblique lighting in each exhibit allows each viewer to read the text describing the relic.

******

In the dark shadows of the garden at The Shetland Art Museum, two figures meet.

"Were you able to get the negatives?"

"No, they weren't at the studio. I was able to get the forensic photos from the plant at the police station."

"Maybe the police have the negatives?"

"I'll have my plant check tomorrow. If they aren't there, I'll check the Hope Ranch on Tuesday night, during the visitation." Both figures leave the garden and join the tour group as they are leaving the museum.

## Chapter Six

The morning breeze stirs the curtains as Emilee and David sit down in their Victorian kitchen. The black and white tiled floor and the black appliances make a beautiful contrast to white painted walls and the cheery, bright colored plates displayed on opened white racks. David is reading the Trevor Times and Emilee is going over her checkbook.

"You know, these articles are really good. This special report on Brent Mathews, is written by Mike Phillips of the Trevor Times."

"Aren't you meeting him today, too?" Emilee asks, as she takes a drink of her breakfast blend coffee.

"Yes, I am. I believe it's later this morning. What are your plans, do you want to meet for lunch?"

"No, dear. Remember, I'm meeting Shannon for lunch. Well, actually, I'm picking her up."

"Oh, that's right, she doesn't have a car, does she?"

"No, she's using Wayne's Charger. But she said she's missing her Beetle. He wouldn't even let her drive yesterday."

"Well, I'm sure she had a relaxing day at home. And they did make it last night."

"Yes. That sure was a shock, huh?"

"Oh, you mean about the break-in and Shannon's hit-and-run?"

"Yes, they have had a bad couple of days." She smiles as she stands and offers David another refill.

"Thanks, but it will have to be my last one, dear. I need to get to the museum."

"Yes, and I have to get down to the bank this morning. I want to get the papers signed on Candlewick Collectibles."

Patting her hand, he smiles at her as he stands up to leave. "I'm so proud of you, Emilee. It's been your dream for many years. You have been a great wife and mother. But I know you want something of your own."

"Thank you, darling. I am excited. I may have to share it with Shannon today."

"I'm sure that would be okay." He takes his coffee upstairs to get ready for his day.

******

Early Monday morning, Chloe opens her eyes to see Tennessee gazing down at her and saying, "Chloe, are you okay? You were crying in your sleep."

She tries to sit up and realizes that she is still encircled in Tennessee's arms. He releases her, they throw off the covers, and each get out on their side of the bed.

Slipping on her robe and slippers, she says, "Yeah...no...I don't know. I'm just so jittery inside."

Tennessee pulls on a pair of work jeans and green tee shirt, and, as he's pulling on his work boots, says, "I'm worried about you, babe, you've had a few bad days."

Walking together, they reach the kitchen where the pre-set automatic has brewed a French- roasted blend of coffee. Chloe pours two cups and joins Tennessee at the table.

Standing beside him, she asks, "What do you want for breakfast?"

After taking a sip, he sets his cup down and replies, "Nothing. I'm meeting Wayne at the bakery in half an hour. "Taking her hands in his and looking at their interlocking fingers, then up into her eyes, he continues, "Why don't you let Shannon and Montana clean up the studio and you stay here at the ranch today? I know how upset you are about this break-in, you can go for a long ride..."

Chloe releases her hands from Tennessee, throws her hands in the air above her head, back down by her sides, and interrupts him, "No, this is important to me. It's *my* studio that was ransacked. I'm going." Putting her hand on his shoulder, in a calmer voice, she says, "Shannon has enough to worry about and Montana has a job to do. Really, love, I'm okay. Just a little shook up, but I'll be fine. I *need* to do this."

Tennessee rises, takes her in his arms, lifts her chin, and kisses her softly. Stepping back and looking into her eyes, he says, "Chloe, I love you. Usually you're like a rock. I'm just worried. Besides, I've been thinking, I'm going to make a few calls. I know Steve is doing all he can with this murder and the rest of this investigation, I think I better take care of this myself."

Looking up at him, she smiles and says, "Really, I'm fine. After more caffeine, a half hour of yoga and a shower, I'll be ready to shoot the moon. I love you, too."

Tennessee gives a little salute to her, smiles and goes out the back door to his burgundy Jeep, and drives into town for his meeting with Wayne.

*I am going to get to the bottom of this, somehow, someway...*

Hearing his Jeep drive away, she pours another cup of coffee and goes into her extra bedroom which she transformed with a ballet bar, a yoga mat and a mirrored wall. Crossing the room, she enters the darkroom, a former walk-in closet with a door, and finds the negatives of the crime scene, and places them into a sleeve. She leaves the darkroom and begins her routine.

Later, feeling rejuvenated, she pulls on a pair of capris jeans and an over-size long sleeve white shirt, rolling up the sleeves to just above her elbows and turns the collar up on the shirt. Choosing a pair of denim ballet-style flats, as she is slipping them on, she notices her pale reflection. She applies a little blusher to her cheeks, sweeps mascara on her long lashes and applies lip gloss to her lips. Brushing her pixie cut, into place, she shakes her head so her hair falls into a natural muss look. Grabbing her bag as she is leaving the bedroom, she enters the workout room and picks up the sleeve of negatives on the table and places them in her bag.

Leaving the house by the garage, she climbs into her Miata and heads into town. Arriving at the police station, Chloe enters and walks down the hall to Steve's office.

Knocking and opening the door, she asks, "Steve, how are you this morning? Here are the negatives."

Taking the negatives from her, Steve says, "Been better, I suppose. I've been getting lots of pressure from the higher-ups to get the relic back to the museum. So, I've been pouring over the report and photos we had taken on Friday. Yesterday, I was looking over the photos and thought I had seen a shadow on a couple of them. I went to see the ones we took Friday, but they're gone."

"Gone, Steve? How can your team pictures be gone?"

"I don't know, Chloe. But I intend to find out." He takes the negatives from her. "But, first things first. Thanks, Chloe."

"No problem. Keep me posted."

Driving the short distance, she arrives at Chloe's Moments Studio and parks her car.

******

Chief Blake leans back in his desk chair and asks the switchboard operator at Precinct 309, "May I speak to Lt. Paul McClintock? Thanks."

"McClintock, homicide."

"Paul, this is Steve Blake."

"Hi, Steve, what's happening? Let me guess, things are so quiet in Whispering Key that you're coming up here to lend me a hand." Paul laughs.

Steve laughs, too. "No, in fact I'm working a murder right now. What I need is to track the sale of one of those disposable phones that was sold in your fair city. I have checked and it was one of four sold at a specific location, can you do some leg work for me?"

"Sure, I'll check it out and get back with you."

Steve gives him all the information he has on the cell phone, then says, "Paul, the sailboat races are starting in a few weeks, we really need you on our team. Will you be able to break away?"

"Oh, yeah! I wouldn't miss it. I'll see what I can find out on this phone and get back with you soon. Talk to you then."

"Bye for now."

******

Mike Phillips pulls his red ponytail back and adjusts the collar of his blue jean, oversize shirt. Tucking it into his boot cut jeans, he sits on the bed to pull on his boots.

*Wayne was really happy with this series I've done on Brent.*

He smiles. Today, a meeting with David Thomas and then, paying a visit to the Mathews home for an interview on their son.

Mike had moved to Whispering Key right after college. He met Wayne Trevor at Florida State, and he and this Texas cowboy felt a kinship from the start. Finding out that Wayne was to become the editor, of the local newspaper was a dream come true. He didn't have the money to belong to the fraternity that all the guys joined. He had to work at a local diner, as a dishwasher, and also at a pizza place down from the campus, a hot spot for the students. He had wanted to belong, but he was glad he made his own way. Being the youngest of three boys, he was also able to make the choice of what he wanted to do with himself in his career. His dream was to be a writer of crime novels.

He stood up and straightened his jeans and stroked his goatee, smiling, yes, he was indeed, a writer. Sitting on his desk was a manuscript of his current work. The names were changed, but the story was the same. His agent wanted the manuscript by the end of the month. They say, write what you know, what you experience. Yes, this was going to be a seller. He knew it.

******

Shannon and Wayne are sharing coffee and Wayne tells her, "I'm meeting Tennessee at the bakery. But first, I have to make those calls."

"Well, I'm going upstairs to get ready. I'm supposed to be at the studio by 9:00."

"Okay." He pulls her up against him, kisses her deeply, and says, "What are you going to do about transportation? I can drop you off, if you want, or you can take my Charger."

"Well, I better take the Charger. I am to meet Emilee at the agency for her to pick me up for lunch. We're having lunch at The Mockingbird Nest."

"You two like that place. A good change of scenery for you, sweet pea."

"That's what I thought, too."As she runs up the stairs, Wayne enters his den to make those calls.

******

Upstairs in her music room, Shannon lovingly strokes her Guarnerius violin with the bow and, as she plays, she feels the tension leave her shoulders and her neck. Another restless night, but this takes her to another place and time...after a half hour she replaces the violin on its stand, and breathing deeply, heads for the bathroom to prepare for her day. She still hoped to get down stairs before Wayne left. Quickly taking a shower and dressing in a pair of capris jeans and a bright orange tee, she slips on her deck shoes, and grabbing her straw shoulder bag, heads down the stairs to Wayne's den.

He was just getting off the phone, smiling at her, says, "I just got off the phone with Darrell he's going to meet Tennessee and me down at the bakery. I got hold of those numbers and Darrell suggested having a party tonight at his place. Some will be here tonight, a few Tuesday."

"Well, that is great, honey. Can I see the list?"

"Sure, I'm going to get a refill, do you have time for one too?"

"Well, no, I better not."

"The list is on the desk." Quickly Shannon copies the names and pockets it in her bag.

Wayne returns and asks, "Do you remember some of them?"

"Yes, some. It's been so long. I bet they've all changed, huh?"

"Oh, probably. I don't think any of us would stay the same." Laughing, "It will be nice to see them, though. Unfortunately, one of those so-called friends is a killer."

Walking over to him, she hugs him and says, "Yes, but we owe it to Brent to find out which one is a Judas."

"I know," patting her hand. "I better get down to the bakery. Did you want to meet later for dinner tonight? I know there will be snacks at Darrell's."

"Uh, no. No need. I'm having a late lunch with Emilee. I'll find something here. There is always leftovers."

"I'll see you later. I'll be home late. You be careful. The insurance agent called and you'll have your car back later today."

"Well, that was fast."

"Yes, only a flat tire and a few scratches. It could have been a lot worse. Promise me you won't do anything crazy. You are driving my Baby, right?"

"Don't worry, Wayne, I'll be careful with *your* Baby!" Kissing him quickly, she leaves and heads to Chloe's.

******

Montana opened her eyes on Monday morning to see the sun rays streaming through her open bedroom window and the sounds of birds chirping and squirrels scurrying up trees behind her little cabin in the woods. Stretching, she climbs out of bed and looks out her bedroom window to the paddock below where her horses are neighing and stomping, alerting her they need attention.

Smiling, she goes down into her kitchen and heads for the coffee pot. Spotting a note beside it, she picks it up and reads:

> *I left early. Lots to do today. Call me later. We'll grab a bite to eat for lunch when you get done at Chloe's. Darrell called this morning and said he's having a gathering at his house tonight. Trish is off, so she's making the snacks. Sounds like a great time. Love you, babe.*

Pocketing the note in her robe, she pours a mug and sits at the table and thinks about her plans for the day. After a refill, she dresses in jeans, an old, plaid shirt of Steve's, and work boots to clean stalls and feed and water her horses. As she is working, she thinks about all that has happened to her family these last few days. The break-in, the trouble for Shannon, and the unsolved case that she's been working on for a while. Is there any connection? Some aspects are the same, but Brent's death, well, that's a different turn of events. Has he been involved? Who killed him? Who broke into Chloe's and followed Shannon? Questions, questions and more questions.

Returning to the house, she quickly does her exercise routine, showers, and dresses in jeans, white t-shirt and tennis shoes, then, grabbing her bag, she heads for Chloe's studio. As she is entering town, she stops by the Cozy Croissants Corner Bakery and picks up croissants, bagels and cream cheese to take over to the studio. She's sure it will be appreciated. She knows she's starving. Arriving at the studio, she grabs her bag and the bakery box and goes inside.

******

David Thomas finished up his morning itinerary and prepared for the interview. Mike Phillips was scheduled in a slot between two appointments. He waited for the first, his old friend, Lorenzo DeLuca. He was surprised to hear from Lorenzo, it had been years. He had met the young man during his own studies in Rome, while under the mentoring of one of the greatest museum curators, he ever had the pleasure of meeting. He was a true mentor, Anthony D'Amico. He met Lorenzo one evening, at dinner, with his wonderful parents, Luigi and Maria DeLuca.

He had been a reserved young man, and very self-centered. Shaking his head, he wonders if the young man had changed. Lorenzo was a teenager then, so changes do happen, anything is possible. He chuckles. Of course, the loss of his mother, Maria, would have definitely caused some changes.

His thoughts are interrupted by a knock on the door. "Come in," David says, as he stands, waiting on his first appointment.

He is startled at the change he sees in the young man before him. He had been a stout young man with a pudgy face and tiny eyes hidden in the folds of flesh. But this young man looked emaciated. He hoped that he wasn't prone to his mother's illness. The young man's eyes were still small, but were deep and dark as his mother's. His mouth had deep lines and it appeared he hadn't smiled in a very, long time. His forehead had deep grooves of wrinkles. This young man had been through a lot and, by his looks, was still going through his pain. Sometimes pain can kill you, and anger, he knew, was deadly as well.

"Hello, Mr. Thomas. I have changed somewhat, but I am Lorenzo DeLuca."

"Ah, yes, Lorenzo, come in. Would you like some coffee or tea?"

"No, no, I'm okay. You probably wonder why I am here?"

"Well, it's been years, Lorenzo. How is your, Dad?"

"Well, we haven't seen much of each other. In fact, Mr. Thomas, I have no contact with him since my mother passed away."

"Well, then, what brings you to visit me? Just dropping by?"

Lorenzo sits down in a chair across from David and crosses his legs, and leans back, crossing his hands in his lap.

"I wanted to see how the museum fared after the hurricane."

"Well, it is okay. The design is the same. Would you like to have a tour?"

"That would be wonderful. I could tell from the appearance outside that there are a few changes, but then, I haven't seen it since college. I came up that one weekend and stayed with you, do you remember?"

"Yes, yes I do. I was surprised you volunteered to stay. Being a young college man. I recall you knew Wayne, Preston and Darrell. Even though you didn't hang out with them very much."

"No, yes, they went to school with me. But, well, that was when Mama was in the first stages of the disease that took her life, within that next few years. "Then, looking over at David, he adds, "I was too far from home, and my father had told me not to bother coming home until after graduation. He suggested you. And well, you were kind enough to agree."

"Yes, your father was a great influence on my life. I was sorry to hear about Maria. She was a beautiful woman. To be taken down in the prime of her life." Shaking his head, he sighs, then adds, "A lot like your fraternity brother, Brent Mathews. Wouldn't you say?"

"Yes, Brent died too soon. Your wife, Mrs. Thomas, is a friend of Shannon and Wayne's, isn't she?"

"Yes, her best friend...I don't think my darling wife knew Brent as well as Shannon and Wayne, though."

"I was just wondering if the police have discovered anything, in the case, yet."

"Well, I know Chief Blake is gathering information and I am sure he will piece it all together before long. I am sure he will get the person involved with this. But, I can't say he's shared what he's come up with yet."

Smiling, Lorenzo stands and says, "No. I guess he will when he's ready. Does he have any leads?"

"No, no. As I said before, Lorenzo, he hasn't shared any with me."

"But he is also working on this theft?"

"Oh, yes, he is. He's a busy man."

"Aren't we all, Mr. Thomas? Well, can we get that tour in? I need to check with my fraternity brothers about plans for the next few days, you understand?"

"Oh, of course. Come, let me lock up here, and then we can get that tour in."

******

Chloe opens the back door to her studio, silently thanking the repairman that installed the new door, Sunday morning. As she passes into the foyer and turns on the lights in the darkroom, the scene from Sunday morning replays in her mind. She picks up the equipment that had been brushed to the floor. Luckily, nothing appeared broken. Leaving the darkroom and entering the reception room in the front, she starts brewing a pot of coffee.

Shannon, comes through the foyer in the back and says, "Chloe, oh, there you are," looking around, "this doesn't look too bad." Moving next to Chloe, she hugs her, "We'll have this cleaned up in no time."

Montana comes in the back door and walks to the front room, "I heard you guys. We'll get to work, but the coffee smells great and I brought croissants and bagels. No cal, of course."

The girls all laugh and enjoy a cup of hazelnut coffee and then get to work.

******

Seated at a round table in the Cozy Croissants Corner Bakery, Wayne's cell phone rings, recognizing the caller, he says, "Hey, Steve, what's up?"

"Wayne, were you able to make that call?"

"Yep! We're here at the bakery, having coffee, why don't you join us?"

"Who's we?"

Wayne chuckles and says, "Darrell, Tennessee and me."

Steve laughs, "I'll be right over."

Wayne tells Darrell and Tennessee, "Steve is on his way." Getting the waitress' attention, he says, "The Chief's on his way, could we get another coffee over here?"

Steve enters the bakery and walks to the table, sitting down, he takes the cup of coffee from the waitress, "Thanks, hon. "Turning toward Wayne, and nodding at the others he asks, "Were you able to get names and numbers?"

"Yeah, I did." Steve pulls a notebook and pen from his shirt pocket and says, "Shoot!"

Wayne takes a notebook out of his pocket and tells Steve, "You already know about Brent, Darrell and me. There are several others, all still alive. Here is the list. I've contacted all of them. Some will come for the visitation and some only for the funeral. A few will be at both."

Darrell interrupts him, "We're all meeting at 8:30 at my place tonight for drinks and catching up. Will you be able to join us, Steve? It may be a great chance for you to check them out."

"Thanks, Darrell, I told Montana I plan on being there."

Standing, they prepare to leave, and Steve pulls Tennessee aside, and says, "Chloe dropped the negatives off this morning. The forensic photos are missing. I'm concerned. Is it public knowledge that Chloe has a darkroom out at the ranch?"

Startled, Tennessee turns to Steve and asks, "Why?"

"I have the negatives, but the perp doesn't know that."

******

Tennessee leaves the bakery and pulls away onto the road back to his place. As he drives through Whispering Key, he spots the girls' vehicles parked by Chloe's Moments Studio. He still was concerned about that text message. He had a few friends that might help him find out who owned the phone. He was sure it was a pay-as-you-go phone. But it had to be sold somewhere.

His cell phone rings as he's pulling in the garage. "Hey, I got that info."

"Yeah, what did you get?"

"The phone is one of four purchased in New York City. The person was unidentified. It was a cash sale. But here's the number. Unless it's blocked, you may be able to find the person."

"Hey, man, that's great. Thanks. Give me a minute, I'm at home now. I'll call you right back when I get inside."

The two hang up and Tennessee hops out of his Jeep and whistles a tune as he enters the house through the garage. Then he dials his friend.

******

Returning to his office, David looks down at his pocket watch and notices he has just enough time for a cup of coffee before his next appointment, Mike Phillips. That was a strange visit with Lorenzo. I need to call his dad and find out why they haven't been in touch. A son needs his father, and a father needs his son, when they're all that's left. Pouring a cup of the deep roasted blend, he sits down at his desk and waits for the knock signifying the arrival of Mike Phillips.

The phone rings and Florence let's him know his 11:00 appointment has arrived. Within a few minutes, he beckons Mike to come in and offers him coffee.

"Thanks, David, that would be great. You know how much coffee we reporters drink. I think we may be in competition with the police."

He laughs softly, and after receiving his coffee, he takes a swallow and then sits down in the chair Lorenzo had just vacated.

"David, I'm writing a series of interviews on Brent Mathews by his friends. I understand that you and he had a business arrangement over the years, he was attending Florida State. Could you tell me a bit about what it was like to work with him?"

Placing his coffee cup on the desk he places a pad in front of him and uncaps his pen. Leaning back in his chair, David smiles and answers Mike, "Yes, yes, I had the good fortune to have him work for me over four years. He had approached me, I guess, it would have been his senior year of high school, and asked if I could be a mentor for him. As you may already know, he was in the band and he had been active in the wrestling and football teams up until then. His senior year, well he was determined to start his path on his future career."

"So, he approached you to be a mentor?"

"Yes, yes he did. It was kind of funny, because Shannon had just begun working with me, as well. She was a sophomore and knew him as a friend of Wayne's. Shannon was not involved in sports or cheerleading, that type of thing. She had continued her studies with her violin and she worked on the school newspaper with Chloe and Wayne, but her heart bent toward more classical things."

"So, did they date?"

"Oh, my, I am sure they went to the local ice cream shop and pizza place, as all the other kids did. But they worked together, really well. I was glad to work with both."

"Did he share his dream of working in the art field with you?"

"Yes, we had many discussions on different artists, but I think, he was more interested in sculptures and relics. I had thought he may follow the path of archeology. I remember his trip with me to Europe. I guess, it would be the summer between his first year of college and his second year. We travelled to some of the sites in Rome and Pompeii. He paid his own way, and he worked really hard, right alongside me and the crew."

Getting up, David refills his coffee cup and offers Mike another refill. Laughing softly, he adds, "I believe that was the same year Emilee and Shannon took that bicycle trip to Europe, too. We crossed paths, there in Italy, and the four of us enjoyed the cuisine of Rome, and also shared many memories of the history and sights and sounds of Italy."

"So, you four enjoyed the sights and sounds of Italy? What happened over the next two years between you and Brent?"

"Well, during the summers, he worked for me and, upon graduation, he started working under me for about a year. During that time he applied for a work program in Italy and France. He left the following summer. And, well, I haven't seen him except on brief trips here in Whispering Key."

"Thank you, David, I appreciate this. I'll have this in tomorrow's edition. My series is only through Wednesday, so I want to top it off with a summary of his life, on the day he will be buried."

Standing up, David shakes Mike's hand, and they bid each other farewell.

******

The girls finish cleaning up the studio in no time flat. Sitting in Chloe's reception room on a cozy, roomy white sofa, the three sisters chat as they sip the hazelnut brew coffee, about the upcoming bus trip and the recent activities that rocked their world since Friday morning.

"Girls, I just wanted to thank you again for the help you both have done here." Looking around her studio, she smiles, relaxing into the overstuffed couch and sips her coffee. "Oh, I know it's not been easy for you, sis. Wayne is still overcome about the whole thing concerning me on Saturday night. I still can't believe all this has happened. It's always someone else and someplace else, you know?"

"I know Tennessee is very upset about the text message from Saturday night. He says he's going to check out some information."

"Well, he should if he can, Chloe. This whole thing about Brent is terrible. You guys had a history with him. That makes it more personal, too." Montana, shaking her ponytail, adds, "Usually, when a crime happens, the police try to narrow down the suspects and then check alibis. But there are no suspects as of now."

"No, there aren't, Montana." Chloe says, stroking the rim of her mug. "The only thing we do have is this break-in, that may produce fingerprints...the text to my phone, the discovery of the ring in my photos, and a shadow Steve remembers from the forensic photos that have disappeared."

"Don't forget Shannon's accident. Steve went there yesterday and checked the paint on her bumper. There was a dark grey streak on the bumper. Do you remember the driver hitting you, Shannon?"

Shaking her head, she takes another sip from her cup and says, "No, Montana, I don't. It's still a blur. I'm remembering, some, as I shared with you yesterday."

"The black crest ring may be a connection. Did Wayne get those names?"

Chloe interrupts. "Yes, he did. I made a copy. Chloe, may I use your copier?"

"Of course. Let's go to my office."

After the copies are made, Montana places her copy of names in her purse and the sisters return to the reception room. Sitting down with another cup of coffee poured, the girls discuss the upcoming trip to St. Augustine.

Finishing their coffee, Montana and Shannon stand to leave and Montana says, "I think some things need to be checked out. So I'll get back to my office. I have some paper work left to do on the assignment I'm working on for Patrick Reagan. Also, I have to get busy organizing a new class on self-defense starting up soon." Laughing she adds, "Oh, by the way, since we are planning on getting away to St. Augustine in a few weeks, I need to get things done for that, too."

The three sisters smile and Montana says, "Steve and I are so looking forward to that trip! I have been trying to pull him away from here for, it seems, forever. Now that Patrick has agreed to come and relieve him, he also assures me he'll keep up on my stuff, too," she laughs. "That will be interesting to see that, don't you think? But he did promise, so I won't worry. Steve and I will be otherwise occupied."

Chloe and Shannon laugh knowingly with their baby sister, then Shannon tells the others, "Yes, to your question, Montana. I need to get busy organizing those plans, too. I'll have it done in a few days, so we each can make our plans. We need time with our men too, lil' sis. It's been too long!"

Chloe stands with her sisters and hugs each one, "Thanks again, girls, doing this alone would have been really hard." She smiles broadly and then says, "I have to finish up some of my work, too. I've got to make a date for a pedicure and manicure next week, so I'll be ready to dance the night away in my Tennessee's arms and play footsies beneath the table, if we ever join you guys for meals." Chloe arches her eyebrows in a Groucho Marx way, and continues, "My plan will be a lot of room service! I may give him a break and go sightseeing and shopping with my two gal pals…,oh, I can't miss taking the black and white photos of the fort..."

Shannon and Montana smile in agreement, pick up their bags from the floor and leave the studio, closing the door behind them.

"Well, she seems like she's going to be okay, eh, sis? I can't recall any time she's been through stuff like this before."

"Yes, I'm sure she's going to be fine. You have a good day, Montana. I'll see you later."

"You have a busy day planned?"

"Yes, I'm going over to my office. I need to line up our reservations." Looking down at her silver watch, she says, "Emilee is picking me up for lunch at 11:00."

******

After Shannon and Montana leave the studio, Chloe pours another cup of the hazelnut brew and takes a much needed break. She was planning on developing those photos from Saturday's bus trip. She also had a list of the upcoming graduates to set up appointments for their Senior Pictures. Since it was a school day, she planned on going down to the high school and set up a table during lunch to make appointments. But, first things first, looking down at her diamond and gold watch, she sees she has time to finish developing the photos from the trip. While the photos are drying, she sits and addresses the envelopes to mail the photo cards. Then, placing each photo in its envelope, she gathers them in a tray and leaves for the post office. Placing the tray in the trunk, she gathers her planner and a stack of business cards and places them into her soft leather tote. Laying it on the seat beside her, she opens the convertible top and with the wind blowing through her pixie haircut and her horse printed scarf flowing behind her, she heads to the school.

******

Blocking his number, Tennessee dials the number written on a piece of paper. The phone rings and the recipient sees the blocked number and doesn't answer. After a few minutes of pacing he dials his partner.

"Yes?"

"We may have a problem."

"Why?"

"I just got a call from a blocked number."

"There is no way anyone could know about these phones."

"Perhaps, but I'm coming to Whispering Key today. I will contact you later."

## Chapter Seven

Shannon is just finishing up the reservations and purchase of concert tickets to a Reba concert that weekend, when the tinkle of the bell on her door alerts she has company.

"Hello, is anyone here?" A male voice calls and she quickly rises and enters the sitting room. In there stand two men. They seem familiar, but then...

"Are you Shannon, Shannon Trevor?"

"Yes, I am. You two are…?"

"You don't remember us?"

Shaking her head, she suddenly smiles and says, "Hello, Charlie Moore and Preston Reynolds. Are you here for Brent Mathews?"

"Well, yes we are. I just ran into Preston down at the Lamplighter Inn where I'm staying. We're on our way down to see Wayne, but we had to drop by and see one of our favorite ladies."

Shannon looks up at both men and notices they have changed.

But then, we all have, she thinks.

"Well, I've been here in Whispering Key for a few weeks. Ginger and I are renovating our house over on Lincoln Drive." Preston explains.

"Oh, why, are you renovating?"

"Ginger and I have decided to open a bed and breakfast and we've been busy. She wants to open it within a few weeks."

"I've been here for a few days. Spending time with my folks." Charlie says.

"Oh, how are the kids and Melissa?"

"Great! Megan and Devon are coming here to stay with Mary Smith and my folks for the summer. You know how grandparents are."

"I do. Is Melissa here too?"

"Not yet. She's bringing the kids in a few days."

"We'll, make sure we get together, it's been awhile."

"Oh, I know she'll contact you before long."

Preston cuts in, "We need to get going, we've got a few things to do before we meet some of the other guys. It's great to see you again, Shannon."

"Yes, you two, too."

As the two friends leave, Emilee comes in, and after a greeting between them, the two friends leave and the two girls are alone.

"Did I interrupt something?"

"No, they just stopped by to say hi. I'll be ready in a few minutes."

"No problem."

Emilee waits as Shannon puts away her work. Then the two friends leave for lunch. Locking up as she leaves, and making sure Wayne's car is locked up, too, she climbs into Emilee's white Sonata. The girls have a pleasant drive on well-kept highways lined by rolling green grass and sweet clover, speckled with homes, horses and cattle.

Located an hour from Whispering Key and on the outskirts of a large metropolis, the Mockingbird Nest was a tea parlor, and bed and breakfast The girls had been frequent visitors and got to know the family. The matron was a connoisseur of tea and her lunches were the talk of the area. Tea was always available, and she offered a lunch menu including a variety of sandwiches, two soup choices, and, of course, small cakes and scones. The special for the day was one of their favorites: French Onion Soup served with shredded cheese and croutons and ham salad sandwiches. After placing their order, the girls sit back and Emilee pours each a cup of tea.

Asking as she pours, "Well, how was it at Chloe's studio this morning? Was it really bad?"

"Yes, the darkroom was a mess. Poor Chloe. But when we finished the cleanup, she was better. We discussed the coming trip to St. Augustine. Are you two coming this time, too?"

"Of course, we wouldn't miss it. There are some antique stores in that area that David and I plan on visiting." Sipping her tea and replacing the Shelly cup in its saucer, she searches her friend's face and asks, "And how are you doing after your accident? I noticed Wayne's car outside your agency. How bad was your Beetle?"

Laughing, Shannon picks up her cup, takes a drink, and swallows before answering. "That might be why Preston and Charlie stopped by. Perhaps they thought Wayne was there." Replacing her Shelly cup in its saucer and moving it aside for the waitress to place their lunches down, she adds, "In answer to your question, my car wasn't damaged too bad. Just a flat tire and some minor damage to the bumper. It's ready to be picked up today. I may check with Wayne and see if he needs his Charger back and if you don't mind, have you follow me to his office and drop me off at the garage."

"No, not at all."

The two girls finish their lunch and, while they are waiting for dessert and another pot of tea, Emilee says, "Shannon, I have some great news for you."

"Oh, really? I would love to hear something positive."

The waitress returns with another pot of tea and a tray of tiny cakes and scones. After she leaves, the two girls make their choices and as Shannon pours the tea she asks Emilee, "Now, don't keep me in suspense. Tell me!"

Emilee takes a bite of scone, and after swallowing, smiles, and squeezes Shannon's hand. "I have signed the papers for my new enterprise, Candlewick Collectibles. Isn't that fantastic?"

Squeezing back, Shannon smiles broadly at her best friend and says, "Yes, that's wonderful. How soon will you open the shop?"

"Well, David and I thought I could make the announcement in a week or so. Please don't let anyone else know yet, okay?"

"Sure, no problem. Is there anything I can do to help? Do you have all your orders completed for your business, you are still planning on selling candles and accessories?"

"Yes, my orders are taken care of and should be here in about a week or so. That's why I'm not making the announcement until they arrive. I figure a few more days, I should have everything ready. I will take you up on your offer to help."

"That's what friends are for," she laughs, adding, "I'm so excited for you. I remember how I felt when I opened my agency, it seems like yesterday. Ups and downs, but it was my dream, and now you'll have your dream, too."

After a few moments of silence, Emilee asks, "Anything new on the relic, or Brent's murder?"

"Well, Steve and Montana have some things they're checking out, but nothing definite. Chloe and I are hoping there will be fingerprints from the break-in at her studio. The crime investigators took all kinds of prints from the studio yesterday. It was a mess, but nothing has been shared with us."

"Well, I hope so, too. I know David is concerned with the return of the relic. He has worked with the museum in Rome countless times since he's been hired as the museum curator. So, he's counting on Steve and Montana solving it. Even though he's my brother, he hasn't shared with David and I, either."

Nodding her head, Shannon says, "We have to trust them, Emilee. I know I would love to get hold of the case and solve it myself." She laughs, "but that's not my job, so I'm told. But I am a woman of curiosity, so if I have the opportunity, you just never know what I might pursue."

Startled at the determination she sees in her friends face, Emilee says, "You'd better be careful, Shannon. I remember how you loved to check things out when we were on the school newspaper, how you felt it was our responsibility to inform our coeds."

"Yes, I did enjoy puzzles, and I was, oh, so nosy." Shannon gently chuckles, "This has got my nose sniffing like a hunting dog on a scent. This has touched my family and me. But, I will be careful."

Giving her friend a knowing loOkay, Emilee warns, "You'd better be!"

The two girls finish their lunch and stand to leave. Taking the bill from the table, Shannon tells Emilee, "This is on me today. I want to check and see if there are any check-ins I need to be aware of, do you mind checking out the gift shop while I do some investigating?"

"Oh, now I get it! You invited me to lunch, your oldest and dearest friend, so you can play detective."

Shannon, nodding at Emilee says, "Uh huh. Do you mind?"

"No, not at all, I'll check out the gift shop, and you can join me when you're finish."

Emilee heads for the gift shop and Shannon heads for the desk.

******

Shannon is glad to see it's one of her friends from high school, at the desk. Clara Adams was a friend from band and had married right after high school. She married and was divorced within a year and now lived alone with her daughter, Mackenzie.

"Hi, Clara, how are you?"

"Oh, hi, Shannon. Did you enjoy your lunch?"

"Yes, as always. I don't think I am ever disappointed."

"That's what we like to hear."

After taking the bill and Shannon's payment, Shannon asks, "Are you guys filled up?"

"No, we don't plan to, until the Sailboat Racing in May. Why?"

"Well, you know Brent Mathews was killed on Friday, and I'm just checking for availability for rooms for some friends that Wayne has called."

"Well, we have a few of those guests already, Ricardo Rossi and Marcus Magliano. Preston Reynolds was here with his sister Ginger, but he checked out today. I guess he's staying with Charlie Moore at the Lamplighter Inn." Looking on the next page adds, "We are expecting Bruce Johnson and Nathan Phillips, tomorrow. But that's about it."

"Well, thanks, Clara. I'll let Wayne know. He's been worrying about making sure they all had rooms. You know how he gets sometimes."

"Oh, yes. I've known Wayne and most of these guys all my life, too. Tell him we'll take good care of them. Okay?"

Smiling, Shannon asks, "How is Mackenzie?"

"Well, we don't get over to Whispering Key much. We'll be there for the funeral on Wednesday, right? She is doing okay, for now. She has finally completed college at Florida State. She is so stubborn, and we've had a lot of disagreements ever since she was a pre-teen. I jokingly told her she's just like her dad. Right now, she wants to get a place of her own. She doesn't want to live at home again."

"Yes, I remember hearing that from our kids, too. Well, I will see you both on Wednesday."

Shannon quickly goes into the gift shop and finds her friend over at the tea cup display.

"Anything?" Emilee asks her.

"Yes, a few are here and a couple are coming tomorrow. Preston was here but checked out and went to The Lamplighter Inn. I guess that's why the two of them were together this morning at my agency."

"Well, let me make this purchase and we can leave."

Emilee goes up to the cashier and they return to Whispering Key.

******

Returning to Trevor Travel Agency later that afternoon, Shannon climbs out of her Beetle and opens the beveled door. Walking into the kitchenette, she makes coffee, and as, the aroma fills the kitchenette, she thinks about what she has discovered, and decides she needs to call Chloe.

Chloe picks up on the first ring. She had been scheduling appointments for graduation photos and, recognizing the caller, quickly answers, "Hey, Shannon. I'm glad you called. I've been so busy this afternoon, graduation appointments, engagement photos, etc."

"I was just calling to see if you were busy. I guess you are."

"No, I just finished scheduling an appointment for later this week. What do you need? I need a break."

"A bike ride."

Moving her feet beneath her desk, Chloe asks, "Bike ride?! You don't mean a motorcycle ride?"

Laughing, Shannon tells her sister, "No, not today. How about joining me for a bicycle ride this afternoon?"

"Sure, I happen to keep my Schwinn down here at the studio. Do you want me to come over to your place about 3:00?"

"Yes, that would be great, I'll finish up here, head home, and meet you there at 3:00. Thanks, Chloe, I have an idea, and I'll tell you then."

"Okay, I'll see you at 3:00."

Chloe hangs up the phone and wonders what that's all about.

******

Chloe arrives on her wine colored Schwinn, climbs off, and puts the kickstand down. She walks up to Shannon's back door and knocks.

"Hey, Chloe. Come on in." Shannon is pulling her chestnut curls in a ponytail. "There's ice tea in the refrigerator and I took out two bottles of water a few minutes ago."

"Okay, how long is this bike ride?" Chloe laughs.

"Oh, not too long, pour a glass of ice tea, and I'll be back in a flash."

Chloe walks over to the glass, door oak, cabinet above the sink and takes out a glass and fills it with ice cubes. Reaching into the refrigerator, she grabs the ice tea and pours a glass. Sipping the berry blend, she takes a seat at the oak table by the window. Shannon comes back in the kitchen, pours herself some ice tea, and sits down across from her sister.

"You probably wonder what this is all about."

Sipping her ice tea, Chloe nods her head and says, "Not that I mind the ride. But I guess it's not to relieve stress, not with everything going on lately. The day is beautiful and I know we could use the exercise. So, what's up?"

"Well, first, I had two visitors this morning. I guess they stopped by because I drove Wayne's Charger today. Perhaps they thought he was there. Anyway, Preston Reynolds and Charlie Moore came by the agency this morning. Preston told me some news I thought you'd be interested to know. Charlie told me Melissa wasn't with him, but was coming later with the kids. But, the interesting thing I wanted to share with you, is that Preston and Ginger are renovating their grandmother's house for a bed and breakfast."

"And how would this interest me?"

"Well, that's not all. Emilee and I had lunch at The Mockingbird Nest and I found out that some of the fraternity brothers were staying there. Ricardo Rossi and Marcus Magliano are there now. Bruce Johnson and Nathan Phillips will be there, tomorrow. But the key is that Preston and Ginger have been staying there, too."

"Well, that is interesting. A bed and breakfast? This ride?"

"Well, I thought we could pay a visit and you could offer to take photos of her renovation."

"I don't think I recall this house. Where is it?"

"Oh, that's the best part. Preston and Ginger's grandmother's house is about four blocks down from my travel agency."

Suddenly, standing up, Chloe takes her glass to the sink and turns and smiles at Shannon. "Little sister, you have come up with a great plan. Let's go!"

Shannon stands and places her glass in the sink and together they head out to their Schwinns.

******

The afternoon breeze gently blows through their hair and both girls are flushed from the fresh air. The whirr of the wheels and the distant sound of the waves crashing in the harbor are the only sounds they hear as they approach the brown and yellow Victorian house.

They turn into the driveway, climb off, put their kickstands down, and they walk around the house. As they draw near the back, they hear the sound of music playing, and the buzzing of a power saw, as they see a single figure bending over a four by four. Immediately they recognize Ginger. They watch a few moments as the tall, lean figure lifts another post and places it on sawhorses. The two girls wait silently until she finishes, looks up and recognizes them.

Smiling, she asks them, "Well, what brings you two here?"

"Hey, Ginger, we were bike riding and we thought we'd stop by and check this out. We heard you were renovating into a bed and breakfast. Wanting to give The Mockingbird Nest a run for its money?" Chloe asks.

"Yes, we are. We're trying not to mess up the main frame and design, but we had to make a few changes. These are going to be used in the kitchen. I have to enlarge the pantry for larger quantities of staples."

"Is Preston here, too?" Shannon asks.

"Well, yes and no. He's been here a bit during the last few weeks. But he's not able to put in as much time as I can. I'll be running it anyway. I guess I'm just getting used to it."

"This looks like a lot of work, Ginger. When do you want to open?"

"Yes, there is a lot of work here, Shannon. But it's been my dream since Grand'Mere passed. I'd like to open in few weeks, Shannon." A few minutes later she offers, "You two in a hurry? I need a break and was just thinking about a tall glass of sweetened, ice tea. Why don't you two come in and have a glass, too?"

The girls follow Ginger to the front of the house and enter the cool foyer. Following Ginger through the dining room into the kitchen, the three girls pour a glass of ice tea and then follow Ginger back to the front. Sitting down on the porch swing, Chloe and Ginger rock gently and Shannon takes a seat on the steps.

"I had a visit from Preston this morning, Ginger. Are you both staying here?"

"No, no we're not, Shannon. We were staying at The Mockingbird Nest and then Preston left I guess there's a party over at Darrell's tonight for the gang. So he's staying with Charlie at The Lamplighter Inn." After taking a long drink of her sweetened ice tea, she adds, "I'm sorry about Brent, Shannon. I know you and Wayne were close to him. He's been working a bit now and then with Preston, so I've seen him occasionally. But I haven't seen him in weeks."

"Thanks, Ginger. I'll let Wayne know. I have a suggestion, Chloe, why don't you and Ginger discuss scheduling some photos of this new venture? While you two chat, can I use the bathroom. Is it right downstairs?"

"Oh, sure, it's at the bottom of the stairs, between the stair well and the dining room."

"Thanks. I'll be right back."

"Now, tell me how I can help you, Ginger." Chloe begins.

"Well, when would you think would be a good time to take the pictures?"

"You only have a few weeks, how about this weekend? Or later this week after you've finished up the pantry?"

"Later this week would be great. This weekend I'm not going to be here." Suddenly, Ginger's phone rings and she reaches in her pocket and answers, "Hi, Ginger Reynolds. Oh, hi, Montana. Tonight? Oh, that would be great. Yeah, I think Preston is having dinner over with Charlie Moore and then they're going to Darrell's party. You'll pick me up. Where will we go? The Oyster Shack? That's great! What time? Okay, I'll be ready. Can you pick me up at The Mockingbird Nest? That's where I'm staying. I'm just about finished here for today." She hangs up the phone.

"Oh, are you planning on going somewhere?"

"Yes, well, Preston suggested I go for a visit with him to Europe. We'll be gone for about week, no more than four or five days. He has a friend that lives in a castle. I've always loved castles. I guess the old princess story has quite the…allure for me."

"Well, I've been to France, I was an exchange student my junior year. And Shannon went on a bicycle tour when she graduated from college. It's a once in a lifetime event. You'll enjoy it."

"I think so, too. I know once I open, I won't have a chance to do much travelling."

Shannon returns, smiles, and looks at her watch, says, "I couldn't help but overhear that, Ginger. That does sound like a great time ahead of you. A castle? Wow!"

Chloe, looking down at her watch, smiles at Ginger and says, "Here's my card, Ginger. I'll call you in a few days and arrange for the shoot."

"Yes, that's great! Well, better get back to work. It's been nice to see you two. I enjoyed our visit."

"We did, too." Chloe says, and then asks, "Do you have time to give us a quick tour? I know you need to get back to work, but that way I could have an idea of what I would want to focus on for the shoot."

"Well, I guess a quick one won't be a bother. Come on."

The girls look at each other, and Shannon nods and whispers, "Good idea!"

******

Monday afternoon, Chloe and Shannon return to the red brick and white Cape Cod and park their bikes against the garage.

The two sisters head for the kitchen and Chloe asks, "Shannon, are you okay? You seem lost in thought. Did you think of something back there at Ginger's?"

"Oh, I'm sorry, Chloe, come on in, we need to talk."

"I'm right behind you."

Reaching the living room, Shannon sits down on the blue and yellow checked couch and pushes aside a bright yellow pillow, leans back and says, "Did you find that visit interesting?"

Chloe, sitting down in a blue checked wing back chair, says, "Yes, the whole thing was informative."

"Well, I have an idea."

"Okay, I'm all ears."

"We need to make a trip back there tonight. Our men will be gone for Darrell's party and, well, Preston and company should be there, too. The only problem would be if Ginger stays and works late tonight."

"Oh, that won't be a problem. You missed the call, Shannon. Montana called and invited her to dinner at the Oyster Shack over near The Mockingbird Nest."

"Oh, I know the place." Clapping her hands in glee, she adds, "She didn't tell Montana we were there, did she?"

"No, but I am sure she will tonight. But, by then, we'll be home. And no one will be the wiser."

"Were you able to search the house while you were gone?"

"Just the lower level. I was afraid to go up the stairs. You know how creaky old stairs can be."

"Oh, yes, we've been caught on them before."

"But, thanks to you, we were able to get a quick tour. "Then moving forward on her chair, adds, "Well, the guys are to be at Darrell's by 8:30, I believe, Chloe. So, call me later after Tennessee leaves. I am sure Wayne will leave early to help Darrell."

"Will do. Until later, then."

"Later, Chloe, and thanks for agreeing to this adventure."

"You better believe it, I am looking forward to it, too."

******

Monday afternoon was coming to a close, another long, uneventful day. Steve Blake walks over to the filing cabinet and begins thumbing through the files laying on top, sorting and filing in their respective drawers.

Michael O'Rourke comes into the office and asks, "Hey, Chief, did you say you wanted me to stop by before I leave?"

"Oh, yeah, Mike, come on in, I want to go over this with you. "Taking one of the files, he returns to his desk. "Take a seat, Mike, is everyone doing okay in there?" He motions to the outer office.

"Yeah, Chief. Rodney and Robin are on the phones and the filing, respectively."

"Great, Mike. I'm glad you have things under control. Now, here are the photos and the transcript for the Mathews case. I would like you to look it over and tell me if you see anything I'm missing. There's got to be something here. You know, I have known you for a long time and I have always thought you would make a great investigator. We'll see what happens, okay?"

Taking the file from Steve, Mike opens and removes the pictures and lays them on the desk. Looking over each one carefully, he says. "I see there is a ring and a chain here, Chief. According to the report from Ralph, there were marks of a chain on the vic, but none found at the scene. I don't remember seeing any in our pics. Also, what's this shadow here? It looks like a figure." Quickly going through the rest of the photos and papers, he looks across the desk at Steve and, searching his face, says, "Where's the forensic photos, Chief?"

"A funny thing, Mike, they have disappeared. When was the last time you looked at them?"

"When you showed them to me, on Friday afternoon. Are you suggesting someone may have removed them from this file?"

Steve, leaning back in his chair and crossing his arms, responds, "Well, Mike, you can tell they're not here. I am going to find out who the crooked cop is in our midst. Don't you think so?"

"Yeah, Chief, I do. I'll keep my eyes and ears open and let you know if I see any funny business. It's got to be done. We have to find out who this is. He/she has to be discovered. You think this has happened before?"

"Well, I 'm going to check into some things, Mike. Okay, that's all for now." Smiling at Mike and shaking his hand, he adds, "Thanks, old man."

Mike leaves and, as he is closing the door, asks, "Do you want me to send anyone else in now, Chief?"

"No, thanks. I'll talk to them myself. I want to catch them off guard. Bye for now, about done for the day?"

"Yes, as soon as I finish up here, g'night, Chief."

"G'night Mike."

Mike O'Rourke leaves the office, and in a few minutes Steve hears him leave the police station. As Steve rocks back in his chair, he thinks, let's see, who do I talk to now?

******

Mike O'Rourke pulls on his khaki jacket and grabs his keys. Heading out to the squad car, he starts it, and pulls out of the parking lot behind the station.

*Now, that was interesting. What is going on? I think I need to meet up with some friends at Madison's tonight, for a few beers and good conversation…*

******

The Artistic License Coffee House was getting ready for the coffee- break rush on Monday afternoon. Max Harris and Mary Smith are sharing their lunch at a corner booth, their last break until they both get to go home.

"How's everything going, Mary?" Max asks, as he is finishing up his cheeseburger and fries.

Shaking out the newspaper, she glances across from him and says, "You have some ketchup on your cheek, Max."

Wiping it away, he blushes and smiles back at her. "Thanks, how is Melissa doing?"

"Oh, okay, I guess. Melissa and the kids should be down here in a few weeks. Charlie is already here. He stopped by yesterday while I was home."

"Devon and Megan will be staying here with me and the Moore's for the summer. The two of them have to find time to get away, without the kids. Being a stay-at-home mom was her choice, but she still needs time with Charlie."

"Are there problems, Mary?"

"I don't know. She doesn't say anything to me about it. She never has, you know. I've left her with her own life. Not always easy, Max. But they don't need an interfering mother or mother-in-law." Shaking his head in agreement, she adds, "The Moores and me are looking forward to the summer visit, too. Those kids are so involved back home, it's been a long time, a year ago, when we were able to visit and spoil them. I think the Moore's spent Christmas with them. I couldn't get away." She softly smiles at him and, looking around, adds, "Couldn't get away from here. I finish my classes at the end of May. I'll be a chef. Don't you miss not having a family, Max?"

"Well, my folks are still alive and I do have two sisters, Amy and Jeni. Jeni has two boys, I really enjoy spending time and playing baseball with them. Amy has no kids, but is busy at school. She graduates this spring, too, with a Bachelor of Fashion Design. You know she's planning on bringing some of her designs for a fashion show in St. Augustine in a few weeks. I told her I would try to be there. I have to see if Melody Smith can work for me that weekend. I am going to check when she comes in later. What are your plans for tonight?"

"I don't have any. When I get off here at 5:00, I'm going to go home and relax. There may be a movie on Turner Classics. If not, I can always go over my homework. You have any plans tonight?"

"Well, I plan on watching the game on the TV at Madison's on the Dock."

"Oh, that sounds like fun. Will you be meeting friends?"

"Yes, a few. Well, I better get back up to the counter, it looks like coffee break time from the hospital has started." Gathering up his lunch, he heads to the back to wash up and wait on the guests at the counter.

As Mary rises to get back to work, too, her cell rings. "Mary, this is Mike, Mike O'Rourke. Is it a bad time?"

"Hi, Mike, no, I mean I am just getting off my break. What can I do for you? Do you need a coffee to be ready?"

"Actually, I wanted to see what your plans are for tonight?"

"Are you asking me on a date, Mike?"

"Well, I guess I am. We talk a lot at the coffee house, and when we run into each other, right?"

Laughing, she answers him, "We have. What did you have in mind tonight?"

"How about meeting me at Madison's? There's a group that will be there to watch the game. I can hold us a table, about 7:00?"

"Well, Max will be there tonight, too. He wants to watch the game on TV. I think it starts at 8:00, so I am sure he'll be there tonight, too. You two can sit and visit until I get there, okay?"

"Sounds great, thanks, Mary. See you then." Mike hangs up the phone.

Walking through the kitchen to the counter, Mary tells Max, "Well, that's interesting. That was Officer Mike O'Rourke. It appears he has asked me for a date. He's meeting me at Madison's tonight. I told him you were going to be there to watch the game, too."

Looking slyly at his co-worker, he smiles and says, "I'll check him for his intentions while we wait."

"Oh, you!" Mary playfully taps him on the arm. Then together they take care of the customers.

******

Chief Blake is heading for his Ranger when his cell rings. Recognizing the caller, he answers, "Hey, Tennessee. What's going on? I hope no new trouble."

"Well, no, not exactly. Steve, I have a friend who found out some information about that cell phone that texted Chloe."

"Well, that's good news. Isn't it? You don't sound too happy."

"Well, I'm not. I dialed the number and it rang through, but no answer. Steve, were you able to find out anything? Do you know where it was purchased?"

"Somewhere in New York City. It was a cash sale. I don't know where or how long ago it was bought. Well, I know some folks up there, Tennessee. Let me check with them and get back to you later. Are you going to be at Darrell's?"

"Yes, I am looking forward to meeting some of those guys. I only know the ones from here, Preston and Darrell. Everyone else is from elsewhere. Did you make any connections from that list Wayne gave you?"

"No. I guess I'll check them out tonight and see where they're staying."

"That's a start. And, how long they've been in Whispering Key."

"Exactly. See you later."

******

Arriving home to change, he sees Montana's Jeep in front of their cabin.

*It wasn't in the garage, I wonder what her plans are? Maybe she and her sisters are getting together. I hope they're not going to get in any trouble.*

Pulling in next to her Jeep, he parks and strides into the kitchen.

Montana is seated at the kitchen table, looking at the photos again.

"What are you doing, babe?"

"Just looking them over, again. I wanted to look at the shadow and see if I could get any detail. He looks like he's tall and slender. I wonder if he's the one that Mary saw Thursday night."

"Well, maybe we should have Mary look at it and see if she can give us a positive ID."

"That's an idea. I called, but she has plans tonight. I do, too."

"Oh, you and your sisters, doing anything special? Dinner or a movie?"

"No, I haven't talked to Chloe or Shannon, babe. But I am taking Ginger Reynolds out for dinner down at The Oyster Shack. She and Preston have been staying at the Mockingbird Inn while they are renovating their grandmother's home into a bed and breakfast. Maybe she can shed some light on how long Preston has been here."

"That would be good to find out. Well, I better get ready. I was going to have supper with you before I went to Darrell's, but I guess I'll grab some leftovers and get changed." Bending down to Montana, he kisses her gently, and says. "I love you, be careful. I'm sure you'll be okay. But your two sisters, well....you understand?"

"Yes, babe. I do, and thanks. Have a good time. Do you want me to wait up for you?"

"No, Montana, that's not necessary. I don't know when I'll be home."

"Okay, babe. I'll see you in the morning."

## Chapter Eight

Monday evening, Max is holding places for Mary and Mike at the bar at Madison's. The game was just about to start and Max had ordered a round of beers for the three of them. Mike arrives first and, looking around, notices that it was another busy game night here at Madison's.

Spotting Max at the bar, he slides on the stool next to him and says, "So, hi, Max. How is it going?"

"It just started Mike. You off for the night?"

"Yeah, the Chief didn't need me. Randy Lewis and Robin Lee are on duty."

"Oh, I know them. They've been here a couple of years. I remember Robin from school. Her brother, Ricky, is going out with my baby sister Amy."

"Yeah, they have. Randy came on board eighteen months ago and Robin just joined the force about ten months ago. You knew her from school? They're here long enough to be able to work on their own. We've all been pretty busy lately with everything going on."

"You know it used to be so safe and secure here at Whispering Key. I guess there are no crime-free towns, huh.?"

"No, crime is everywhere." Shaking his head, he smiles and takes a drink of his beer, saying, "Man, this hits the spot."

Then, wiping his mouth with his hand and watching the wall-mounted TV, he observes the area and the folks that are regulars. He met many of them in his time here at Whispering Key. His thoughts are interrupted by Mary climbing up on the stool beside him.

"Well, hi, guys! This mine?" She gestures as the bartender places a frosted glass in front of her.

"Yep, it's yours. Max bought this round, drink up, the next round is on me."

Mike smiles. The three friends enjoy the game and the evening.

During halftime, Mary tells them, "I'll be right back."

While she's gone, Max orders another round, and the two men talk about the game. In a few minutes, Mary returns and climbs back up on the stool.

"So, tell me, Mike, what brought you to our fine town?"

Laughing, Mike tells her, "About five years ago I was working on the New York City police department and I had been assigned a security detail at an annual conference of a five star hotel chain. The executive, Charlie Moore, and I met, and each year I was called to work the security detail. It was great. Luckily, no problems. But over the years, we became close."

"Charlie Moore? My son-in-law?"

"Yes, the son of Ron Moore from the Lamplighter Inn."

"Wow, that's interesting, Mike. But you still haven't told me how you came to be here?"

Taking a swallow of his beer, wiping his mouth and smoothing his goatee, he tells her. "Charlie's dad came one year and was introduced to me. Ron had heard of an opening with this police department, so he invited me to come for a visit and to talk to Chief Steve Blake."

"Oh, I see, and apparently Steve liked you enough to hire you?"

"Yep, the rest is history."

"Did you ever meet my daughter Melissa?"

"Oh, yes I did. In the beginning, she travelled with Charlie. Then, I guess, when the kids came along, she stayed home with them."

Nodding and finishing her beer, she says, "Yes. Megan had some issues when she was small, and well, to make a long story short, Melissa felt she would do better with home school. Then Devon arrived about ten years later. They had a miscarriage between them. I guess Megan was about six and then, four years later, Devon arrived."

As the game started up again, Mary excuses herself again and, on returning, tells Mike, "Mike, do you see the table in the back? The corner table? I thought I recognized a man at the table."

"Where?" Mike asks and adds, "Where did you recognize him from?"

"From Thursday night at the Artistic License Coffee House. I worked that night and waited on him and Brent." Removing her cell from her bag, she begins to make a call, telling Mike, "I have to call Steve and let him know. I've never seen him before and not since, until tonight. He's still in town, and Steve needs to know."

Softly, he places his hand on hers and says, "Mary, Mary! You have already told the police. Remember I am the police?"

"Well, you're right. I just don't want him to disappear."

"Don't worry! I'll follow him when he leaves, and I'll let Steve know where he's at, okay?"

Glancing at the table one more time, Mary nods at Mike. Smiling down at her, he pats her hand and tells her, "Now, let's finish watching the game." As he orders another round for the three of them.

******

Montana pulls in front of The Mockingbird Nest, and Ginger, watching, comes out.

"Hey, Ginger. How's it going?"

"Been busy. I really need this break."

"Me, too. I've been working so hard lately."

"I never knew how much work is involved in renovating a Victorian house. It's been so long since I've been able to shop for me."

Looking over at her, Montana says, "It's been a long time for me, too. There's a new shop in Whispering Key Mall, have you had a chance to check it out?"

"No, what kind of designs do they carry?"

"If it's fashion, you'll have to check with Chloe. I prefer shoe shopping. This shop has it all!"

"That sounds great. I'll have to check it out before I leave for Europe."

"Europe? How are you so lucky?"

"Preston wants to take me to Europe before I open the Gingerbread Inn. He's promised me a tour of castles that are hundreds of years old."

Montana says, pulling in the parking lot at the Oyster Bar, "A trip to die for!"

The girls laugh and enter the restaurant. After ordering their drinks and dinner, the girls sit back and relax as they wait for their drinks to be delivered.

Ginger, opening her napkin and placing it on her lap says, "It was so good to see Shannon and Chloe this afternoon."

Swallowing her water, Montana asks, "Oh, they came by today?"

Excitedly, Ginger tells her, "Yes! Chloe is going to help promote the Gingerbread Inn. She's suggested taking photos for my brochures."

"Well, that sounds great. Chloe knows her stuff. How long have you and your brother been renovating?"

As their drinks arrive, Ginger answers, "Preston's been in and out of the area for the last few weeks. I've been doing most of it myself."

Laughing, Montana says, "Isn't that like a man?"

The girls share a smile as their oysters arrive.

******

Tennessee swallows the last bite of his Pecan-Crusted Tilapia, and says, "That was delicious, Chloe. What are you going to do while I'm at Darrell's tonight?"

Standing up to clear the table, Chloe answers, "Um...probably watch a movie or something. Don't worry about me, I'll be fine."

Taking the serving plates to the kitchen counter, Tennessee sets them down, leans against the counter, and says, "Chloe, I'm worried about you. That guy knows who you are, your phone number, where your studio is, and probably knows where we live. He killed Brent, he committed murder, he ran Shannon off the road. I don't know what I would do if something happened to you."

"I'll be right here, I'll lock up when you leave, I'll be fine. Don't worry, just go to Darrell's and have a good time. Who knows, maybe you'll find out something that will lead to this person's arrest."

"Speaking of learning something. I did find out about the phone that texted you, it was bought in New York. I've given the info to Steve, maybe he'll be able to track it. If you think you'll be okay, I'll go, but if you need me just call."

"I'll be fine. Tell Trish hi for me, and I'll call her next week for an appointment. Don't worry, just have a good time. Love ya, Tennessee."

Looking down into her eyes he tells her, "I love you, Chloe." Kissing her softly, he releases her from his arms and heads for the garage.

******

Joining Trish in the kitchen, Darrell kisses her cheek and says, "Babe, you've gone to a lot of trouble." He looks at the kitchen counter with hors d'oeuvres on platters.

Trish smiles and says, "Even your favorite, crab cakes. "Then she adds, "Help me take these to the family room. I already have ice and cold drinks at the bar."

As they take the platters into the family room the doorbell rings. Darrell returns to the kitchen and lets Wayne in the door.

"You're the first one here," Darrell says.

"Good! We need to talk about, what we need to do. We have to get the guys from out of town talking about where they've been, and what they've been doing."

The doorbell rings again and, as he turns to go to the door, Darrell tells Wayne, "Good. I'd like to know that, too."

Darrell leads the way to the family room followed by Charlie, Preston and Wayne. "The bar is open, help yourselves. The hors d'oeuvres are on the table."

Wayne picks up an appetizer and Trish enters with Marcus Magliano, Ricardo Rossi, Steve and Tennessee.

"Help yourselves to drinks and food, guys. How about a game of pool?" Darrell racks up the balls and chooses a cue stick from the wall, then asks, "Any takers?"

Preston takes a cue stick from the wall and approaches the table and says, "It's been a long time. Do you want to play Eight Ball or Nine Ball?"

"Let's play Eight Ball." Darrell suggests, then, to the others asks, "Everyone have what they need?"

Everyone nods yes.

Wayne picks up an appetizer asks Ricardo and Marcus, "So, tell me what have you two been doing since graduation?"

"You're a newspaper editor, aren't you, Wayne? How long have you been doing that?" Preston asks him from across the pool table as he bends to take his shot.

"Well, I took over the business, I guess, about five years ago. Dad is still around, but he has left it up to me. All that training has finally paid off and Dad is active in retirement activities." He chuckles.

"Well, I've been working in Europe." Marcus states. "I work with a museum in Rome, Paris and London. I've even been to Germany. I've had an interesting life. Your wife, Shannon, she's been doing some work with the museum in town?"

"Yes, she has. She's a great person, I'm lucky to have her. Are you married or do you have a…partner?"

"No, no one could keep up with me. I get out once in a while, but nothing serious." Marcus says.

"And how about you, Ricardo?" Wayne asks.

"No, I don't have a significant other, either, "He laughs. "No one could handle me, I can be very demanding and, with my career in the art world, I can't settle in one place. That usually is an important thing for most women...how do you say, security?"

"Do all three of you work together?" Darrell joins in the conversation.

"Yes, we do. I work with Marcus and Preston occasionally, too." Ricardo answers him.

"How about you, Charlie? What have you been doing?" Wayne asks.

Charlie replies, "I've been into promotion."

Steve asks, "What kind of promotion? Retail, manufacturing, or business?"

Charlie laughing says, "All three! I do promotion for my chain of hotels."

"Hotels?" Tennessee asks, "Any in Europe? Preferably France? Ever since Chloe went to Paris, she's wanted to go back. Any in Paris?"

Charlie smiles, "Yes, I remember Chloe's trip. I think it was our junior year. She was a different girl when she returned. Yes, I have one near the Louvre."

Preston picks up another appetizer and smiles, "Your wife, Trish, sure has gone to a lot of work here tonight. Is she usually so gifted? Some men have all the luck, beautiful wives and terrific cooks in the bargain."

"Yes, Trish is that." Darrell smiles. "I guess I'm lucky."

Ricardo goes to the bar and mixes another drink. "Where is that lovely lady?"

"She's in the kitchen, watching the cooking channel. She spends a lot of time there, when she's home. You know she has her own beauty shop downtown, right down from The Artistic License Coffee House. Have you guys had time to go there yet? On Friday and Saturday nights they have folk music and jazz/blues karaoke."

"Yes, we saw that earlier, when we arrived in town." Marcus tells him.

"No, we haven't yet. I am sure we will, though, before we leave later this week." Ricardo adds.

"Well, how about another game, who's next?" Darrell asks.

"I'll play Wayne," says Preston.

"Okay with me," Darrell laughs and joins Charlie on the couch and starts to fill a plate of hors d'oeuvres. "I need to get my strength up."

Laughing, Steve, Marcus, Ricardo and Tennessee start a game of poker.

Wayne chooses a cue stick and racks the balls asking, "What's your game? Eight Ball or Nine Ball?"

"I got a run on Eight Ball, let's play that." Preston suggests as he lines up his shot.

******

After Tennessee left, Chloe finishes loading the dishwasher and runs down the hall to their bedroom to change. Glancing at the alarm clock on the table beside her bed, she sees that she has only fifteen minutes before she is to meet Shannon at Ginger's. Calling Shannon, she tells her she's running a little behind, but will be leaving in a bit. Hurriedly, she dresses in black jeans and a long sleeved black polo shirt. She grabs her pen light and lock picking kit, goes to the kitchen and picks up her cell phone, keys, grabs her black hobo bag, and enters the garage. A few minutes later, she finds a parking spot on the street one block down from the home that will soon become the Gingerbread Inn. Taking the pen light and lock picking kit from her bag, she puts them in the pocket of her jeans She stows her handbag in the trunk, locks the Miata and walks quickly to Ginger's. Trying to stay in the shadows, Chloe arrives before Shannon, and waits for her under the cypress tree in the front yard at Ginger's.

******

Shannon, hanging up the phone on her bedside table, begins dressing for her investigating trip to Ginger's with Chloe. Tonight, Wayne and Tennessee would be otherwise occupied, and Montana was conveniently out of the way too. She had unknowingly provided them with the convenient removal of Ginger. Montana and Ginger were going out to the Oyster Bar, an out of way place about an hour from Whispering Key.

Chloe and her should be finished by then, and safe at home, she hoped. Pulling the long-sleeved black tee shirt over her dark curls, she smooth it over her dark jeans, and returning to her closet, chooses a dark pair of running shoes. She smiles, as she remembers an experience with her gal pal, Emilee, that most of these old homes had an attic door that could only be opened with a skeleton key. Pocketing the key and placing a black cap on her curls, she checks in her bag for cell phone, keys, flashlight, and white gloves, and runs down the stairs to the door.

Leaving a light on, she locks the door and runs to her Beetle, just returned that afternoon. She was glad she didn't have to drive Wayne's Charger. Backing out of the drive, she drives the few blocks to Ginger's house. Chloe was meeting her there. As she approaches the neighborhood, she dims her lights, and slowly pulls into a parking place a block away. Not giving herself a chance to change her mind, she climbs out, grabs her keys, flashlight, white gloves, locks the car, and slowly makes her way up the street to the Victorian house, once owned by Preston's and Ginger's grandparents.

Staying in the shadows, she spots Chloe standing beneath the cypress trees away from the streetlights, she walks stealthily toward the figure in the shadows. Waiting a few minutes to make sure no one else is around, the two women walk slowly toward the massive house with the wraparound porch. Following the narrow sidewalk, they walk around to the back of the house.

Moonlight shines on the two sawhorses and the board that rests on them, blocking access to the porch. Skirting around them, they stumble on the steps which are loaded with tool boxes and electrical cords. Chloe's foot catches under a cord and she loses her balance. Grabbing her elbow, Shannon helps her right herself.

Finally, reaching the door, Chloe reaches into the pocket of her black jeans and pulls out her case of lock- picking tools. Holding her flashlight above the handle, Shannon waits as Chloe chooses a pick and slides it in the lock. Carefully, listening to the clicking of the tumblers, the lock opens. Together, the two sisters slide through the door. The windows are bare of curtains and moonlight shines in, as Chloe pockets her case, and with the help of the moonlight, they move through the layout of the first floor. Chloe leads the way down the hall to the staircase in the foyer. Reaching the staircase, they stop, wait and listen.

Then, slowly, they climb the steps, remembering from their earlier visit, which steps creaked, they climb up the stairs, and reaching the second floor, listen to the stillness surrounding them. The windows are bare of curtains upstairs, too. The doors leading off the hall are open and they peak in them as they walk from room to room. They notice that each room has furniture covered with dust cloths. The bathroom is painted and a new toilet and vanity are installed near the claw-footed tub. Slowly, they continue down the hall.

At the end of the hall is a closed, locked door which leads to the attic. Shannon pulls the skeleton key from her pocket and inserts it in the ancient, locked door. The two exchange a smile as it unlocks the door. They pull at the door handle and it creaks open. Glancing around fearfully, the girls stand quietly and hold their breath. Nothing breaks the stillness. Slowly, they mount the stairs, occasionally a step creaks, they stand motionless for a moment, and then they continue moving up. Chloe, leading the way, arrives at the top. She notices a small dormer window on the wall overlooking the front of the house and a skylight in the ceiling. The musty smell and the heavy dust tickle their noses and they both stifle a sneeze.

Shannon nudges her to move forward and together they stand at the top of the steps and look around the attic. The moonlight streams through the skylight and they quickly begin going through boxes, pictures, and furniture surrounding them, stuff they can open or move. Chloe discovers an old sailor's chest and excitedly points it out to Shannon.

Kneeling down beside it, Chloe starts to check for panels and latches to open. Then, pulling out the case of picks once more, she chooses one and carefully inserts it, it doesn't click. She tries another and it doesn't work, either. Shannon kneels beside her and, taking the case from Chloe, hands her the last one. Frantically, Chloe tries to insert it, and fumbling drops it to the floor. Using her flashlight, Shannon helps her sister locate the pick and Chloe slides it into the lock of the chest and they hear a click. At the same time they hear voices coming up the stairs.

Staring at each other, they exchange a look of fear, they are in danger of getting caught. Holding their breath, they wait to see if the owners voices notice the attic door ajar and climb the attic steps. The girls listen as two male voices discuss...

"I just wanted to look at it once more. I wanted to caress it with my fingers. I want to take it with me now!"

"No, we have to wait. Everything has to be right. I thought I saw a light earlier. I can't think of who it would be, but maybe we do need to go up and see."

"Yes, yes, my friend. We need to make sure. The jeweled cross must not be discovered."

The girls suddenly realize they are alone with two unknown men, and looking around frantically, seek some place to hide. Suddenly, they hear a ringing of a phone.

"Yes. Okay. We're on our way."

Chloe whispers, "There are two, Shannon!"

Shannon nods her head and, placing her finger to her lips, sliding her hand across her neck, lets Chloe know she should be quiet. Not moving a muscle, they wait.

The two male voices continue, "We need to get going. We will be missed, and I still have to make that stop."

"Let's go. We are expected elsewhere. You're right, I'll have it soon enough, my friend."

The girls listen as the men turn from the door and descend the stairs, their voices fading. Waiting a few moments, Chloe lifts up the lid of the chest and begins removing some items and places them on the floor. Photo albums, boxes, and then, she sees it, a velvet covered item. Lifting out the item, she unwraps it and, looking across at Shannon, gasps in surprise and pleasure. Shannon pulls out a pair of white cotton gloves and hands them to Chloe, while she puts on another pair. Then Chloe unwraps the treasure, the jeweled, cross relic. The moonlight casts an eerie glow on the jewels and the two girls gasp at its beauty.

Quickly, Shannon starts to return each item back to the chest and realizes that Chloe is still holding on to the last item. The relic.

Chloe pulls it to her chest and shakes her head, her wide hazel eyes reflecting in the moonlight beaming down from the skylight, and whispers to her sister, "No, we need to take this to Montana. We can tell her where we found it and she can get a warrant We can't leave it now that we've found it."

Shaking her head, Shannon whispers back, "No, Chloe. We can't. Remember, we are in the act of breaking and entering. Like what happened at your studio. She can't get a warrant. But we do need to tell her about our discovery. We need to let her know that Preston has to be involved, too!"

Unwillingly, Chloe returns the relic to the trunk and Shannon repacks the other items around it, then closes the trunk and it locks. Standing up, Chloe removes the gloves and hands them to Shannon. Making sure nothing looks disturbed, the two girls leave the attic. Chloe takes a moment and looks out the dormer window overlooking the front of the house and sees two figures walking out to the street. One figure walks with a certain gait.

Shaking her head, Shannon asks her softly, "What is it?"

"I saw two figures leaving here and one walked with a familiar gait."

"Oh, maybe you'll recall where you've seen it. Was it Preston?"

Shaking her head, Chloe leads the way to the stairs. Before descending the attic stairs, they wait in silence. Quickly, they run down the stairs, with the moonlight guiding them, following the hall into the kitchen, and carefully skirt around the items in the kitchen.

They see headlights reflect on the walls in the kitchen, standing in the shadows, they wait. Holding their breath, they listen as the engine stops and starts up again and slowly backs up, exiting the driveway. They stand very still for a few more minutes, listening for the return of the car. After a few more minutes of silence, they leave the house by the back carefully skirting the tool boxes, electrical cords, and finally the two sawhorses.

Staying in the shadows and the cover of the cypress trees, the two girls run to their cars and, after a quick hug, look around again, to be sure no one is watching and waiting, they start their cars and, with dim lights, head home in opposite directions.

******

Pulling in her garage, Chloe climbs out of her Miata and slowly gathers her stuff, and looking around, walks to the lighted doorway. Unlocking her door, she steps into the security of her home. Closing and locking the door, she walks to her kitchen for a much needed cup of coffee. Pouring coffee into a blue mug, she saunters down the hall to the den. Turning the light on as she enters and moving slowly to her tan recliner, she stretches out and brings her mug to her lips.

Her thoughts return to finding the relic. It was so beautiful! A real treasure! She was so glad they found it. Preston or Ginger had to be involved...remembering watching those two men walk down the drive...she knew she had seen the walk of the one man, where had she seen him before?

She feels a sudden chill, rubs her arms and, finishing her coffee, takes her cup to the kitchen and places her mug into the dishwasher. Thinking she should call Montana, glancing at her watch, she realizes Montana could still be with Ginger. She smiles, Montana would be upset about their little escapade tonight. Tomorrow, she and Shannon would have to tell Montana about their discovery. If she told her tonight, she wouldn't be allowed any sleep, she laughs gently to herself. She leaves the kitchen light on for Tennessee and drags her weary body to her bedroom, for a hot bath and bed.

She hoped Tennessee was having a good time. Maybe he'll discover something, too! As her thoughts return to Ginger's, she wonders again, who were those two men? Shaking her head, she enters the bathroom and runs a hot, relaxing bath. Climbing out of the tub, she dries off with a thick towel and wraps it around her. Stepping into her bedroom, she pulls on a pair of olive green pajama shorts and a matching camisole top and climbs into her king size bed. Snuggling beneath the wine and green quilt, as her head finds the pillow, she thinks, oh, yeah, the visitation's tomorrow...

******

Arriving at home, Shannon unlocks the brick red door, and closing it behind her locks it securely. Flipping the lights on as she moves through her Cape Cod home, she enters the kitchen and turns the burner on beneath the deep red teakettle. As she waits for the comforting whistle, she sits down at her oak table, looks out the window scanning the night sky and, spotting the moon, she sighs, and recalls each moment of their adventure at Ginger's. Lost in thought, she hears the whistle and brews a cup of tea. Taking the tea with her, she passes the den and notices the light blinking on the phone, alerting her of a message.

Pressing the button, she hears Wayne's voice, "Well, babe, you may be in the shower, or hopefully, by now, in bed. Just wanted to let you know I've discovered a few things that you may find are interesting. I know how your curious mind works, "He chuckles softly, "But I just wanted to tell you I love you and will be home late. That seems a lot lately. Sleep well, my sweet pea. No need to call back."

Shannon pushes the erase button and slowly climbs the stairs. Choosing a hot shower over a bath, she moves beneath the pulsating jet stream from the shower head, and feels the tension and stress leave her body. Drying off with a fluffy towel, donning her pajama shorts and tee shirt over her wet head of curls, she turns down the quilt and sheets, fluffs her pillow, lays her head down, pulls the blanket up over her shoulders, closes her eyes and thinks.. she should look at those pictures, and her surveillance video...again… they need to share their discovery with Montana...maybe Chloe will remember who one of those men were...

******

Arriving at his room he dials the familiar number.

"Yes?"

"We may have a problem."

"Another problem?"

"I was told the waitress recognized our friend from Thursday night."

"You know what has to be done."

******

Ending the call, he begins pacing the floor in his hotel room, thinking…

*Who do I have working with me, a bunch of idiots?...Earlier at the house, was someone else there?...Who could have been there?...Did they find my treasure?...I should have taken it with me. Now, I need to wait a few more days…a few more days…I'll be back at my castle…I must be patient… It will be over in a few more days…*

# Chapter Nine

Shannon, at her agency on Tuesday morning, picks up the phone, dials the hotel in St. Augustine, and reserves a section of rooms for her tour group. The hotel chain has worked with her many times and she is a valued customer. Standing up, she stretches and decides a cup of tea is in order. She has had a busy morning. When she arrived at the agency, there were client calls to return. Then she made reservations for the Reba concert and dinner for Saturday night with Wayne, Tennessee, Chloe, Montana, Steve and her. She also reserved a carriage ride to follow. Now, she completed the hotel reservations.

Everything was settled. She sighed, as she waited, while a cup of tea brewed. Her thoughts returned to last night. Chloe said the one man's gait was familiar, but she couldn't remember anything else. Placing her cup on her desk, she sits down in her chair, she rocks, and remembers last night at Ginger's. Remembering the fear of discovery by the two men who showed up and her sister's indisputable claim, she picks up the phone and dials Chloe's cell.

Cheerfully picking up the phone, she says, "Hi, Shannon! How are you today? Have you been able to keep your mind on business?"

"Chloe, is there a chance you can come over here to the agency?"

"Sure, what's wrong?"

"I was just thinking about last night and what you said."

"Oh, do you mean about that guy? I still don't recall who it is."

"I need to show you something. It may jog your memory."

"Sure, be right there. Do you still have those photos I gave you or do you want me to bring mine over?"

"Okay, uh...bring them, too. I'll see you in a few." Shannon carefully inserts the video tape and, within moments, the image appears. Rewinding it, she shuts it off and waits for Chloe.

"Hey, I'm here, Shannon."

"Come on back to my office, Chloe. Lock the door before you come back here, okay?"

Chloe closes the door and locks it, then walks through the sitting room into Shannon's office. Coming into the office, she says, "I'm here." Noticing her sister's pale face, she quickly adds, "Hey, what's the matter?" Pulling a chair over to sit beside Shannon, she sits down and looks at the screen.

"Chloe, I want to show this to you. I installed a surveillance camera and it recorded this."

Chloe asks, "A surveillance video? How did forensic miss it?"

Smiling at her sister impishly, Shannon says, "Well, it was hidden. I placed a copy of my Cape Cod house as a birdhouse, beneath the upstairs kitchen window. It hides the camera during the daylight hours. At night, it runs quietly, it is motion-activated." She begins the video, saying, "This is not something you'll want to see. But I think you need to. It may help you identify this unknown man."

Together, the two sisters watch the last moments of Brent's life. The ladies watch the replay of the night Brent was killed by someone who they both recognized. The screen before them portrayed Brent being followed by two other men. They could only observe them from the back. The tall man had a gun on Brent, he stood shoulder to shoulder with Brent, and the shorter man walked with a gait of a crippled man.

The tall man shoves Brent beside the garbage dumpster. The shorter man removes a tool from his own pocket, grabs the briefcase from Brent's hand, and snaps the chain with a pair of wire clippers. The chain and another shiny object fall to the ground. While the tall man holds the gun against Brent's back, the shorter man removes the key from Brent's pocket and unlocks the briefcase.

The girls watch in wonder as the briefcase is opened. The velvet cloth that they had seen the night before is unwrapped and the jeweled cross glows in all its beauty. Rewrapping the cross, the man removes it from the briefcase, and lovingly caresses it just as Chloe did the night before. Chloe and Shannon continue to watch as the man holds the wrapped relic to his chest and steps back, nodding to his companion.

The ladies watch in horror as the man holding the relic uncovers it again and, with hard thrusts, shatters the back of Brent's head. In terror, the sisters watch Brent fall lifeless to the ground beside the dumpster. Quickly rewrapping the relic, closing and leaving the briefcase, the two men back up and disappear from the camera's eye. The girls rewind the tape and sit in silence as each recalls each moment of the scene.

"Oh, my gosh! Shannon, what are we going to do? We just saw the killing of our friend."

"I know, Chloe, I have watched this a couple of times before and I am still overwhelmed with the whole terrible scene. That's why I wanted the photos, so I could see if I could identify one of these men."

"Okay, well, let's go over them now. Do you have coffee made? Maybe with a cup of hot java, we will be able to get somewhere."

Taking their coffee, the two sisters return to the sitting room, sit down on the Queen Anne sofa and Chloe lays the photos out on the coffee table. They examine each photo.

"You know, Shannon, I recognize the gait of the shorter man. I haven't seen him in a long time, but I think it's someone I knew in France. Oh, it's been so many years. Do you have the list of those guys that attended Florida State with Wayne? I want to check it again."

"Of course, Chloe, let me go get it."

Shannon returns with the list, hands it to Chloe, she quickly reads it and, then, shaking her head, says, "There's someone missing. Are you sure you got all the names?"

"I believe so, Chloe. Maybe we should call Montana and share what we have."

"Yes, we need to. Do you want me to call, or you?"

"I'll call and see if she can come over." Shannon picks up her cell and dials Montana. "Montana, hi. Chloe and I want to share with you some things we discovered."

"Oh, okay, sis. I see your calling from you're cell, are you at home or in your car?"

"We're here at the travel agency. We'll be waiting for you in the sitting room."

"I'll be right there."

Montana arrives a few minutes later.

Chloe answers the door and tells Montana, "I'm locking the door, so we won't have any interruptions. Get a cup of coffee, and join us in the sitting room."

"What are you girls up to?"

"Get your coffee. I think you'll need it."

Chloe joins Shannon in the sitting room. Going by way of the kitchenette, Montana pours a mug of coffee and joins her sisters.

Shannon asks as Montana enters the sitting room and sits down in the wing back chair, "First, do you remember the list of members Wayne gave to Steve?"

"Yes, Steve shared them with me, there were ten that joined that year."

"Ten? I only have nine." Shannon tells her.

"Well, Shannon, I have it with me." Reaching into her purse, she removes the list and hands it to Shannon. After viewing it, she gives it to Chloe. "I guess I missed the last name."

Chloe, looking up from the list at her two sisters, says, "Yes, that's him, Shannon. The one with the gait. I remember him from France."

Montana, looking from one to the other says, "Gait? France? What's going on here?"

Placing her mug on the coffee table, Shannon pulls the tape from her pocket and looking over at Montana, says, "First, I have to tell you. I installed a surveillance camera behind this building a few days ago. I know I should have turned it over before, but I guess so much was going on, and then my accident, well I just kept forgetting."

"Well, you have had a lot going on, Shannon. Are you telling me this tape has Brent's murder on it?" Taking a drink of her cup of coffee, Montana asks, "How did you hide the camera?"

"Beneath the kitchen window upstairs. I made a copy of my house, the size of a birdhouse, and placed the camera there." Nodding at her younger sister, and with a steady gaze from her wide, dark eyes adds, "That's not all, Chloe and I had an adventure last night. While you had dinner with Ginger Reynolds...well, we," pointing to Chloe and herself, "decided to check something out. You tell her, Chloe."

"Yes, well, we went for a bike ride yesterday afternoon, and stopped to talk to Ginger. I used the excuse that I was offering to help her line up photos for her brochures."

Nodding, Montana says, "Yes, Ginger mentioned your visit. I was surprised, but I assumed it was as innocent as you just said." Looking from one of her older sisters to the other, she leans back and adds, "Go on."

"Anyway, Montana, Shannon and I returned last night to their house and discovered something we know you need to know."

"Okay...? You two better get the story out and fast."

"Well, we…we kind of committed an unauthorized search." Shannon tells her, then adds, "During our uh….our search, we discovered the relic."

"The relic? Oh my gosh! Where was it hidden?"

Chloe quickly interrupted, "It was in a sea-man's chest. It was a real treasure, in a treasure chest. There were photos and other memorabilia, too, but it was somewhat buried beneath all that."

"You two not only made an illegal search, did you remove it, too? And your fingerprints? Oh, what did you two get yourselves into now?" Standing up, Montana begins pacing back and forth.

Looking at each other, then, standing tall, both girls tell her, "No!"

Then Chloe says, "No, Montana, we didn't remove it. I wanted to, but Shannon told me I couldn't."

"And we used white gloves I brought with me, Montana. Our fingerprints won't be there and they're definitely not on the relic."

Still pacing back and forth, Montana says, "What about this gait? And the names on the list?"

"Shannon showed me her list and she must have missed the last one. I recognize the last name, because I ran into him during my time in France. It's been years and he was a lot heavier, then."

"In France, during the time you were an exchange student? I remember that time. Didn't Mom alert a girlfriend of hers about your arrival?"

Nodding, Chloe smiles and says, "Yes, his mom was that lady. She invited me to dinner many times. And I spent some time there on weekends, too."

"Last night, while we were there at the Reynolds house, we thought we may have been discovered. We knew that Preston should have been at the party, and later, we discovered that he was. So the two men we saw were not Preston and a friend." Shannon explains and adds, "The gait was what Chloe observed, when she looked out the attic window as we were getting ready to go, and the two men were leaving."

Chloe chimes in, "We couldn't identify the men, Montana, but that brings us back to this tape Shannon has. You better show her, Shannon."

"Yes, 'come into my parlor, said the spider to the fly'." After viewing the video, Montana says, "I'll show this to Steve. "Then, looking over at Shannon, adds, "This could be why you were run off the road."

******

Shannon arrives at The Lamplighter Inn about 12:45 on Tuesday afternoon. She takes a seat in a comfortable, striped, wingback chair, and places her Vera Bradley shoulder bag on the floor beside her. At exactly 1:00, Mary Mathews strolls through the double doors and, spying Shannon, briskly walks over to her.

Shannon stands and, after a brief hug, Mary says, "Shannon, dear, you look lovely, like the deep magenta rose I have on the patio. That deep pink is a is a wonderful color for you."

Shannon, taking her arm, thanks her and, together, the two ladies walk into the dining room. The cherry wood furniture is polished to a deep shine. The tables are set with the finest china and crystal and the owners, Ron and Betty Moore, mingle with their guests. The waiter greets them and shows them to a quiet corner table for two, and pulls out their chairs. He fills their glasses with sparkling water and lemon, and takes their drink order.

"It's so good to see you, again, Charles. Tell your folks hello from me."

Nodding, he says, "Yes, we are all sorry for your loss, Miss Mary. Brent will be missed by many. Tell Doc our thoughts are with you both."

"Yes, I will, thank you." Placing her bag on the floor, she smiles over at Shannon, and says, "It's so good to see you, dear. I am so glad you called. We haven't seen each other like this in a long time."

"No, we usually meet for lunch on a more regular basis. I'm glad we have the chance to do so again." Placing her linen napkin in her lap, Shannon adds,

"You look fresh as a sun kissed daisy. I love that shade of yellow on you. Miss Mary, it gives you a sunshine glow."

Mary smiles and looks up as Charles returns with two frosted glasses of sweetened ice tea, and places them on coasters in front of them.

Susan Moore approaches their table. "Hello, Miss Mary and Miss Shannon. Our special today is a ham and cheese quiche and your choice of tossed salad or chilled, yellow squash soup. Or would you care to view the menu?"

"The special sounds good to me, Susan, with the chilled, yellow-squash soup. How about you, Shannon?"

"Um...yes, that does sound good. I'll have the same, Susan. Thank you." Susan leaves to submit their order and Shannon continues, "Miss Mary, I was wondering why Brent didn't take us up on our offer. Why did he choose to stay here?"

"Well, Shannon, the museum made the reservation for him and they were going to pick up the tab. Besides, dear, there is more security here. Your apartment, although I am sure it's lovely," she pats Shannon's hand, "Doesn't have that. The same reason he didn't stay with us."

"I see. Well, I guess it's because of all the other art thefts over the last year. They have to be careful."

Their chilled soup arrives and the two ladies begin eating their meal. Susan lays a basket holding a variety of crusty rolls and butter in the center and assures them their ham and cheese quiche will be up soon.

After a few moments of buttering their rolls and eating, Mary asks, "He was found behind your agency, wasn't he, Shannon?"

"Yes. It still makes me tremble. Him, lying there beside the dumpster."

"I wonder if he knew who they were? The Chief said he was supposed to meet your sister, Montana, on Thursday night. I guess we'll never know his last moments, Shannon."

Their quiche arrives and the conversation goes on to happier topics.

"Shannon, Doc and I have talked and we were thinking it might be fun to get away on one of your bus tours. Do you have many left?"

Shaking her head and breaking open another roll, she spreads butter on it and answers, "No, our last one is coming up, Miss Mary. We are going on a trip to St. Augustine in May. I've already booked rooms at the hotel where we stay, let me know as soon as you can, so I can set one aside. I think it would really do you both some good. A change of scenery would be a great way to take your minds off all of this. There will be carriage rides, shopping, and even a fashion show, this time."

Laughing, Mary tells her, "It sounds like a great time. You don't have to talk me into it. I know since Doc has retired, we've talked about doing some trips together. This would be a great opportunity and we'll be with you and Wayne."

"Yes, along with Chloe, Tennessee, Montana, and Steve. It will be great for all of us."

"Do you have a lot of folks signed up?"

"Quite a few, I am sure you and Doc will know them. I believe Ron and Betty Moore were the first ones to sign up." She chuckles. "They usually are my first clients on every trip."

Smiling, Mary says, "Yes, they would be. They always enjoy an adventure. Their grandkids are coming this summer. So, I think they're glad you don't have trips then. You never know what they might miss." She laughs softly.

Mary and Shannon set their soup bowls aside and Susan quickly removes them.

As they continue eating the delectable ham and cheese quiche, Shannon asks, "How is your gardening going?"

"It's so relaxing and the garden is looking so lovely right now. But the weeds seem to pop up daily. I love to spend time out there. It gives me such a sense of accomplishment. Have you been able to work in your garden?"

"Some, but I usually don't get to it every day. Usually I work out there on weekends, and I try to get to it a couple of nights a week. Sometimes, Wayne works late, and, well, I'll eat something light and quick and take advantage of those evenings."

"Yes, I remember those times, too," patting Shannon's hand again. "Before you know it, though, he'll be retired and the two of you will have plenty of time together."

Squeezing Mary's hand back, "Oh, I know, Miss Mary. Sooner than I think. "Then she adds, "So what do you plan to do this afternoon?"

"Well, I've decided to visit the nursery in town. I'm thinking of replacing some flowers with a gold fish pond. Doc and I have a place to sit and spend time together in the garden. We do a lot of eating on the patio. But I know Doc wants to get his hands dirty." She laughs and Shannon laughs, too.

# Chapter Ten

Tuesday evening the sun is still bright, and the breeze is blowing gently. The Andrews Funeral Home is packed with family and friends of Brent Mathews. The building was built in the 1800's and, as was the tradition of days gone by, the upstairs were the living quarters and the downstairs was the parlor and business side of the home. Darrell and Ralph Andrews were raised in this house and, then, when Ralph moved out and Darrell married Trish, it was no longer the same. Their parents moved to a smaller home and Darrell bought a house at 210 Sycamore Lane.

Mike and Mary Mathews were standing beside their son in the Rose Room. Visitors shared stories of Brent from his boyhood, high school wrestling, and basketball memories. Their son also had a reputation as a winner in sailboat racing. Coaches, teachers, neighbors, old girlfriends, and classmates came through, and shared their condolences. His fraternity brothers came through, too. Some of them only knew him in college, others from high school. They all had met Dr. Mike and Mary Mathews, at one time or another. Mary was a tall, matronly woman, with silver hair, and warm brown eyes. Dr. Mike was tall also, and had a silver moustache that matched his silver hair, his twinkling blue eyes, even in sorrow, were full of warmth and tenderness.

Wayne and Shannon Trevor stood beside the Mathews and shared memories about Brent, too. It was a memorial to show sorrow over the loss of Brent, but it was also a celebration of all he was.

Ricardo Rossi, Marcus Magliano, Bruce Johnson, Nathan Phillips, Preston Reynolds, and Charlie Moore came through together. As they leave the funeral home, they meet Darrell, and tell him that some of them are going to Madison's for a drink in Brent's honor and some are going sightseeing. Arriving at Madison's, the three enter and take seats at corner table made from cypress wood. The bar was a common hangout for the residents of Whispering Key. Each year, beginning in May, there is a constant gathering of sailboat enthusiasts who participate in racing.

"Well, the visitation went well, don't you agree?"

"Yes, our Brent was well-liked, but not so well-known, hey?"

"I can remember many of the things shared tonight. But after our community hero left, nobody is aware of the double-life he led."

"Nobody knew the criminal side of Brent Mathews."

The three nod in agreement. Then two others join them and the conversation continues.

"Were the photos found? Or the negatives?"

"No, I don't have them yet."

"Well, we know what has to be done."

"Yes, I'm on my way."

******

After the visitation, Mary Smith turns the key in the lock of her small cottage on the outskirts of town. Entering the living room, she slips out of her heels and hangs up her jacket on the coat rack inside her door. Bending down, she picks up the mail that has fallen through the, slot in her door.

Patches her cat, winds around her legs and Mary strokes her, and the low roar tumbling up from within lightens her heart. "I know. I'm late with supper. Come on, you, follow Mom."

Mary places the mail on the table beside her faded, wingback rocker. She heads into the kitchen, opening a can of cat food and placing it on a small plate, and sets it on the floor beside a small bowl of kibble. After refilling the water bowl, she returns to the sink and fills her teakettle with water for a cup of tea. her nightly ritual. Looking around, she sees her books on the shiny maple dining table and sighs as she remembers she has to finish up a recipe for her class.

Turning back to the stove, she looks over at the school pictures of Megan and Devon hanging on the refrigerator, her pride and joy. She was so looking forward to seeing them this summer. Melissa would be bringing them here in a few weeks. School would be done and she would be graduating. Melissa was bringing the kids with her, to help her mother celebrate the new adventure of her life. It sure took a while to accomplish it.

As she is thinking about her daughter, her thoughts recall the visitation. Doc and Mrs. Mathews losing their son, Brent...she shivers as she thinks...how hard that must be...how would she be able to go on if something happened to her baby girl. The whistling teakettle interrupts her thoughts and she brews a cup of tea and returns to her rocker.

After placing her tea on the table on a doily, she picks up the mail and flips through it. Thumbing through the expected bills, she finds two letters. One from her best friend, Bonnie Mattern, out in Texas. Happily, she puts it on top of her bills, she wants to sit back and drink her tea with this one. Then, she looks down on the other one, no return address, with her name printed out in letters clipped from a newspaper. Taking a letter opener from the table, she slides it through the envelope and unfolds the paper inside. The same type of letters spell out a warning:

“DON'T BE A STOOL PIGEON!"

On the bottom of that page was pasted a picture of a dead pigeon with a noose around its neck and a knife protruding from its chest with, what looked like, drops of blood speckling the feathered breast. Standing up, the letter drops to the floor, as she covers her mouth with her hands. Glancing to the floor, her mail has landed on top of the awful picture. She fumbles in her slacks pocket for her phone. Trembling, she dials Chief Steve Blake's cell number from her contact list.

As she hears it connect, she quickly speaks into it, “Hello Chief, this is Mary...Mary Smith. I need to tell you...I need you to come here...right away..."

"Hey, slow down, do you need to call 911? Are you hurt? Where is here?"

"I...I have a letter. I think someone knows...I'm at home...can you come...please, Chief, please!"

"Knows what? I'm on my way."

Steve pulls in front of Mary Smith's rural home. He quickly runs up the cobblestone path to her door. She is standing in the doorway, watching for him, holding a piece of paper.

"I was checking out a prank call at the high school. So I just happened to be in your neighborhood."

He follows her into her house and sits beside her on the faded, blue sofa. She hands him the paper in her hand and he reads it.

"When did you get this?"

"I have my mail delivered here, through my door. Tom Stevens, the rural mailman, doesn't mind delivering it to me here. I was told I should have a mailbox. I keep meaning to rent one at the post office. Well, in answer to your question, I must have left for the visitation before mail delivery, I had no mail until I came home. Just now."

"Is this all you have?"

"No, the rest of my mail is bills and a letter from my friend in Texas. Do you still have the envelope?"

"Yes, yes, here it is." She hands him the envelope. Then she asks, "Do you think it could be related with what I told Mike O'Rourke about the identity of that man at Madison's?"

"I haven't talked to Mike. Were you able to ID someone? What did you tell him?"

"Yes. I saw the same man who met Brent on Thursday."

"Then, yes, I would say it is related. Will you be okay here tonight? Do you want to stay in town?"

"No, I have Patches and I'll be fine. Do you think you can check for prints on this?"

"Yes, I'm sure I can. At least I'll try. If you're sure about staying here, make sure your windows and doors are locked. I don't like that mail slot in the door. You really need to block that and make other arrangements for your mail."

"Yes, I will tomorrow. Thanks, Steve, I appreciate this."

"No problem. Now I'm going to check your windows and back door. You lock up the front door when I leave, and I mean this, if you hear anything or smell anything funny. Get out of here and call 911. Okay?"

"Yes, I will." After checking the windows and back door, Steve leaves and waits until he hears the deadbolt slide on her side of the door.

******

A car is parked up the road from Mary's house. The lights are off and the motor is silent. The driver watches as Chief Steve Blake leaves Mary's house. Smiling, he waits. Well, I guess she didn't listen to the warning. Oh, my, Mary. What have you done? Shaking his head he says, "I guess you need to be taken care of..."

******

After a lull in the visitation, close to the end of the evening, Shannon pours Wayne a cup of coffee and, returning to the Rose Room, hands it to him and asks, "How are you doing, hon? I know it's been a long day for you. You holding up okay?"

Wayne smiles at his wife and, taking the cup from her hands, nods tiredly at her. "Thanks for this. I think I need to take a walk and get some fresh air."

Shannon takes his hand, squeezes it and agrees. Walking together, they head for the door, where Darrell is standing. He sees the two of them approaching and nods in their direction. "That's what I need, a cup of coffee. It's been a long evening."

"Shannon and I are going outside for a few minutes, then I'll relieve you. Will that be okay? Or do you need it now?"

"Okay, that sounds like a great idea. Oh, by the way, the fraternity brothers came through and some said they were going over to Madison's for a brew in his honor. It was sure good to see them, you know. So many memories…"

"Yeah, it was. But now, one of them hides the heart of a Judas and a killer. Do you think Steve needs to be told this?"

"Yeah, I do. I haven't seen him yet, but, when I do, I'll let him know. Now, go out for that walk and get back in here, that coffee sure smells good."

Wayne lifts his cup in salute, nods his head, smiles at his friend and, taking Shannon's hand, says, "I'm out of here. Be back in a few minutes."

******

Mary double checks the doors and the windows. She lets Patches out the back door and waits in the lighted doorway. Within a few minutes, Patches returns and she locks the door. Sitting down in front of the TV, she turns on the Turner Classics. After having a dish of caramel praline ice cream, she takes the bowl into her kitchen and places it in the dishwasher. Years ago, Melissa used to complain about having to do the dishes by hand. When she married Charlie Moore, they gave her a dishwasher for her birthday that first year. She still smiles at what Melissa had told her, 'Mom, now we're like everyone else.'

She starts up the dishwasher and turns off the lights. In the morning, she'd put everything away. She was just too tired, to wait for it now. Heading into the bathroom, she emerges a few minutes later and prepares for bed. Patches jumps on the queen-size traditional bed, and Mary pulls up the log cabin quilt to snuggle beneath and, within minutes, both are asleep.

******

Later, as Shannon is adjusting the black cameo on the tie of her blouse, Montana enters and joins her at the sink in the ladies room. Shannon opens her jade clutch, removes her comb, and combs her hair.

Montana applies lip gloss and then smiles at her older sister, "Have you seen Chloe?"

"Earlier, Tennessee and Chloe came through the line. I think they are both still here. Is Steve with you? Have you been here long?"

"Not long, and no, Steve isn't here yet. I'm just worried about her. You know, Chloe has always been our rock. This break-in on Sunday and, then, your adventure Monday night has shaken all of us."

Shannon nods and says, "Montana, can we take a walk? I need some fresh air."

Looking cautiously at Shannon, "Sure, let's go."

As they head outside, the evening twilight has given way to moonlight, and the soft, night breeze gently musses their hair as they stroll the garden path behind the funeral home. Reaching a bench, they look around and sit down.

"Did you have a chance to go over what Chloe and I showed you this morning?"

"Yes, I did. I shared it with Steve and he wants to wait until he gets those prints back from her break-in on Sunday. Steve was called out on a prank call out at the high school, just before we came here, so he had to check it out. He should be here soon."

"Well, I'm sure Darrell or Wayne will tell him when they see him, but, in case they don't, I wanted you to know that the fraternity brothers were here and left. Some went sightseeing and the others went down to Madison's for a brew in his honor."

"Well, thanks, sis. I appreciate it. I know we're checking out all of them thoroughly. There must be a connection. But we need to find out which are involved and which aren't. One, Lorenzo DeLuca, was also a brother, but he's not been seen. I think I remember him, I know his dad. I've worked with him."

"Do you think this man might be him?"

"I'm not sure, Shannon. I'll let you two know as soon as I know."

"Okay, I guess I'll have to wait, too. But, I'm so impatient. I want to get this settled now."

Patting her sister's arm, Montana says, "I know, sis, I know! Now, let's go find Chloe and I sure could use a cup of coffee."

Together, the girls rise and return to the funeral home. Entering into the funeral home, they see Tennessee leaving the family room, "Hi, girls. Chloe is in the family room by the coffee. You know how she enjoys her coffee!"

"Yeah, we do, Tennessee, it's a family trait. You know what they say, don't stand between a girl and her coffee."

They laugh and, together, the girls go into the family room and over to the bay window where Chloe is standing, looking out into the moonlit garden.

Holding a cup of coffee, she turns around and says to her younger sisters, "I saw the two of you walking in the garden. I bet it's nice out there. "Turning from the window, she adds, "So what's up? You two look like you have something to share.

Shannon and Montana pour a cup of the hazelnut coffee. Montana chooses a cookie and places it on a napkin and they join Chloe on the rose brocade couch.

"Just what I need." Montana says, after taking a sip of the brew.

"Yes, we do," Shannon says, as she takes a sip of her coffee. "Perhaps it's nothing, but then there are so many possibilities. This case gets stranger and stranger. Earlier, the fraternity brothers left together but separated at the parking lot. Some went sightseeing and some went to Madison's to share a brew in Brent's honor."

"All the fraternity brothers came except for Lorenzo DeLuca. Do you remember him, Chloe?"

"Yes, I do. He wasn't one of our classmates here, but, he was one of the gang at college. His dad was with Interpol, wasn't he?"

"Yes, I have worked with his father a few times, as has Patrick and Steve."

"Yes, as I told you earlier, Montana. Lorenzo's mom was our mom's friend."

Nodding, Montana says, "Yes, she was. I remember mom and dad had arranged for you to have someone there in case you needed them. You even stayed with them a few weekends, too."

"Yes. It was nice to have someone there." Smiling she adds, "I think Lorenzo had a crush on me."

"Did you date him, Chloe?" Shannon asks.

"No, he was too shy to ask. I just knew. He was always so accommodating. Why do you ask, Montana?"

"Well, Chloe, he's the only fraternity brother that hasn't made an appearance. Did Wayne tell you whether he was coming or not, Shannon?"

Standing up, Shannon returns their cups to the kitchen and tells her, "No, I don't remember him telling me anything. He just said that some were coming in on Monday for the party and the rest were coming on Tuesday for the visitation. All were going to be at the funeral."

As the girls leave, Montana says, "Well, I guess I'll have to wait until tomorrow to check on him."

******

The cell phone rings. "Well, did you take care of it?"

"No the negatives weren't there."

"You didn't set the alarm off during your visit?"

"Of course not. I am very careful. I broke their code and was able to get in there with no problem."

"Did you speak with our friend at the police department? Was he able to get the surveillance video?"

"I don't think so. We may have a problem there, too."

"Well, I think a stern warning to Miss Chloe is due."

"I'll take care of that tonight."

"Yes, tonight. It's getting a little tighter. We better move up the arrangements. I will keep in touch."

He closes the cell phone and returns it to his pocket. Looking around his room at the Lamplighter Inn, he stretches out on the bed and smiles as he thinks about the jeweled cross. Soon it will be in his hands again, this time not as a murder weapon, but a priceless relic.

*As it should be, these imbecile fools, working with them has become a problem. It's time to part ways. I won't need them anymore. Just get through tomorrow.*

*Brent was a problem. Darrell did a good job on him, though. And the turnout, well, his reputation still stands. His family was always good to me when I visited. Now, if these fools could only complete this job...well, I'll be on my way.*

******

Steve returns to the funeral home and spots Tennessee and Chloe.

Approaching them, he also sees Darrell and Wayne, Darrell greets him and says, "Hey, Steve. I'm glad you got back here. I wanted to tell you that the fraternity brothers left earlier. Some of them went to toast Brent. Some went sightseeing. They assured me they would be here in the morning."

"Thanks, Darrell. I need to speak with Chloe and Tennessee. Excuse me." Joining Tennessee and Chloe, he tells them, "Hey, you two, I was just down at AAA Alarm Company. I was checking out a prank call from the high school. Some kids were playing around. Stevens told me you two had another break-in, this time at Hope Ranch. The alarm didn't go off at first. This guy is a professional. He somehow figured out your code and deactivated it. You'll need to talk to Stevens about resetting your pass code.

I thought you two might want to come with me to the ranch and check things out. I am sure it has to do with your negatives, Chloe. We want to be sure, though."

Chloe begins to tremble and Tennessee wraps his arms around her and says, "You're right, Steve, we need to get back home. Can we ride with you, we'll pick up our vehicle later. I am sure Darrell won't mind."

"Sure. Here comes Montana. I'll see if she can come, too. Hey, babe, I have to take Tennessee and Chloe to the ranch. There was another break-in. Do you want to take Chloe and follow me?"

"Sure, babe, I will. Come on Chloe, my truck is a lot more comfortable than Steve's squad car."

Wrapping her arm around her older sister, she walks with her to her Jeep Liberty. "Hey, now, I am driving the Bronco tonight." He smiles at her and adds, "But she will be more comfortable riding with her sister, Let's go folks."

As they climb into Steve's Bronco, his phone rings, "Blake here."

"Hey, Steve, this is Paul McClintock"

"Yeah, Paul. What did you find out?"

"Those phones were purchased in New York City at a drug store, cash sale, there were actually four purchased. I got the print-out of the calls made and they began about a year ago. This Mathews murder case, and the missing cross, may be connected to other art thefts." Wow! How many have been reported?"

"In the past year, three known thefts have been reported. One in Italy, one from France and one from a museum in England. There may be another from Germany, that's still under investigation."

"Wow! Were they similar items?"

Paul leans back in his chair at his office in New York City, and tells him, "All are one-of-a-kind art treasures."

"I have a contact at the police department in Rome. I can ask him if he has received any alerts about the thefts."

"Let me know what you find out and I'll do the same." Paul replies.

"Will do. Talk to you soon." Steve answers, and ends the call.

Pulling into the circle drive at Hope Ranch, Steve and Tennessee jump out of the Bronco. Montana pulls in beside them, and the two girls hop out and run over to their men. The flashing lights of two squad cars reflect on their faces as they run to the house. Entering through the back door into the kitchen, Steve leads the way down the hall to Chloe's exercise room. While Steve talks to his forensic team and two of his officers, Chloe walks into the room followed closely by Tennessee. Chloe walks to her ballet bar and sees her reflection in the mirrored wall.

Tears begin to fall as she sees her favorite chair and table knocked over in the reflection. Lying beside the chair is one ballet slipper. She turns and walks over to her chair. Tennessee helps her set it up and the table, too. Chloe picks up the one ballet slipper and looks up at Tennessee with a look of an unspoken question.

She turns away, still clutching the slipper in her clenched hand, and goes beyond the forensic team to her darkroom. Once again, everything is cleared from the workbench and equipment and trays are on the floor.

Tennessee walks up behind her and pulls her into his arms, whispering, "Chloe, it's only stuff. It can be replaced."

Chloe tries to smile back at him, but her lips only tremble. Still clutching the one ballet slipper, Chloe lets Tennessee lead her out of the room, down the hall and back to the kitchen. They walk over to the kitchen table.

Pulling the chair out for Chloe, Tennessee asks, "How about a cup of coffee?" Looking over at Montana, he asks, "Montana, would you start a pot? Stay here with her, I'm going back to check things out."

Nodding, Montana prepares coffee, and Tennessee joins Steve in the darkroom.

"Is this the only room damaged?"

Steve places his hand on his shoulder and says, "No, the safe in your bedroom is standing open and the papers are scattered on the floor. You'll need to check to see what's missing. The perpetrator may have only been searching for those negatives. You'll have to let me know if anything else is missing."

Proceeding to the bedroom, Tennessee scans the room. Paintings are removed from the walls and randomly tossed and the safe door is open.

Steve, coming up behind him says, "The forensic team has finished in here for now. You can see if anything is missing."

Tennessee bends over to pick up papers, deeds, jewelry and cash. Nothing was missing. Shaking his head in disbelief and turning to Steve, says,

"They didn't even take the money!"

Nodding his head, Steve tells him, "It wasn't what they wanted. Those negatives were all they wanted and they weren't here."

The two friends join the girls in the kitchen and Steve suggests, "Why don't you two gather some things, and come to our place? You can get this cleaned up tomorrow after the funeral and I know you'll sleep better away from here tonight."

"Sounds like a grand idea, Chloe, a slumber party." Looking over at Steve, she hugs her sister and adds, "Tomorrow will be soon enough to tackle this chaos."

## Chapter Eleven

Arriving at Castlekeep Ridge, Steve unlocks the door and Chloe and Tennessee follow Montana into the kitchen.

"How about some hot cocoa?" Montana offers, as she fills the copper teakettle and turns on the stove.

"That sounds good. Let's go in the den, and I'll build a fire."

Chloe sits on the love seat and Tennessee wraps an afghan around her trembling shoulders. Bringing the hot cocoa into the den, Montana sits next to Chloe and sets the tray of mugs on the coffee table.

Steve's cell rings, "Blake here."

"Steve, this is Darrell. How are they doing?"

Steve replies, "As expected. Do you have the pallbearers lined up?"

"I have Wayne, Charlie, Preston, and Bruce. Do you think you and Tennessee could be the other two?"

Tennessee interrupts, "I'll do it."

Steve answers Darrell, "Yeah, we will. What time do you need us?"

"9:30, okay?"

"We'll see you then." Steve closes his phone.

Warming up, Chloe removes the afghan and sits up on the edge of the love seat. Taking a sip of her cocoa, she asks Steve, "What did you guys find out last night?"

"It seems that they have been in the cities where other thefts have taken place. I need to make some calls."

"I'll refill our cups." Montana suggests, as she gathers the mugs and heads for the kitchen.

Standing up, Chloe says, "I'll go with you."

Looking up, Steve tells the girls, "Wait, I'm going to call Luigi."

"Luigi, this is Blake."

"Steve, anything new?"

"Did you receive an alert about an art theft in Munich?"

"Yes, that makes four thefts from museums in the past year."

"Make that five."

"Five?"

"We have reason to suspect that the robbery and murder here is tied to the others."

Startled at the news, Luigi comments, "Keep me posted. I will do the same. Any leads, I'll let you know. None of the other thefts included a murder."

"Well, this time we have reason to believe that this turn of events may not have been planned. But it turned another page and this one, if proven, will be more costly for those involved."

"Ciao for now."

"Later."

As Chloe is heading for the kitchen with Montana, her cell beeps, alerting her of an incoming text message. Opening her phone, she reads the message. Chloe drops her phone and Montana reaches her as her knees buckle beneath her. Helping her sister to the table, Chloe sits down, and Montana noticing her peaked face, calls out for Tennessee and Steve. The men run to the kitchen and, as Tennessee's long strides reach his wife, Montana picks up the phone and hands it to Steve.

Steve looks down and reads aloud, "If you value your life, give me the negatives. More to follow."

******

Over at 224 Lilac Lane, Wayne arrives home from the funeral home and drops his keys on the marble counter in the kitchen. He notices the coffee pot is on and pours himself a cup of coffee. Taking the cup to his den across the hall, he enters and goes over to his desk. On the top of the desk, Wayne finds his notes for the eulogy tomorrow.

He thinks to himself, Oh, I have to finish that, too. What am I going to write down. So many unanswered questions. Were you involved, Brent? Did you know who killed you? What were your last thoughts? Did you know you were leaving us, were you going to miss us? As we miss you?

Glancing outside the bay window, he notices the streetlights glowing. The night turned out to be pleasant, so far, but he knew the gentle whispering of the breeze forewarned there may be a slight storm tonight.

He thinks, it matches my mood.

Glancing up, he hears Shannon coming down the stairs.

Coming into the den, she stands and looks at him and says, "You look downcast. What's on your mind?"

Looking at her, across from him in her apricot robe and her tousled hair, he smiles, "You know, you always look good to me. Even after crawling out of bed."

He puts out his hand and beckons her to join him at his desk. Bending down to kiss his head, she strokes his cheek and asks, "What's wrong, babe? You look like you've been through a rough time, did you have any trouble coming home?"

Pulling her onto his lap, he nuzzles her and answers, "No, no trouble there. Just, I don't know what to write on this eulogy, I promised the Mathews. It's amazing that sometimes you just don't know what your so-called friends end up doing." After a few moments he adds, "By the way have you heard from your sisters? The Hopes had another break-in, this time at their ranch."

Surprised, Shannon asks, "Hope Ranch, are Tennessee and Chloe okay? Was anything taken?"

"Oh, yes, honey, they're fine. They weren't there, thank God. Steve didn't tell us if anything was taken, they headed out there. Tennessee and Chloe are staying with Montana and Steve tonight. You can call them in the morning."

"Phew! I will go out there in the morning. But tell me, what did you find out last night?"

"Just that four of them have been working at the same museums and, it appears it has to be one of my 'frat brothers' who killed Brent."

Kissing his forehead and sighing "Oh, Wayne. I know this is hard on you. I know the truth will come out. I'm sorry it happened."

Hugging her, he picks up his notes for the eulogy, lays them back onto his desk, and taps them with his fingers, "This, I have to finish tonight, any suggestions?"

"What do you have so far?" Shannon picks up the notes and reads silently to herself. "Why don't you just recall the times when you were boys and high school pals? I don't think anyone will expect anything after college. You guys all went separate ways after graduation, right?"

"You're right, sweet pea. Thanks." He gives her a kiss goodnight and sends her off to bed. "I'll see you in the morning, okay? I love you, goodnight."

Giving Wayne a hug, she says, "I'll see you later, I love you, too."

After climbing the stairs to their bedroom, Shannon sits on the four poster bed, picks up the phone from the bedside table, and dials Montana at home.

Picking up the receiver in the kitchen and recognizing the caller-ID, Montana answers, "Hi, Shannon. Chloe is here with me. I'll put you on speaker."

"Chloe. How are you?"

"I'm doing much better, Shannon."

Shannon asks, "What happened tonight?"

Montana, filling the mugs, says, "Hope Ranch was broken into and Chloe and Tennessee are staying with us tonight. Steve thinks it may be related to the photos."

Chloe adds, "The theft of the relic and Brent's murder may be tied to a ring of art thefts."

Shannon, pulling her feet beneath her on the bed, agrees, "David has shared with me the alerts he received about three art thefts in the last year, one in Rome, one in Paris and one in London. Are there any others?"

Montana answers, "Steve just got off the phone with Luigi. There was also one in Munich."

Chloe says, "Tennessee shared this evening that some of the frat brothers have been working at several museums. He said that they have been to Rome, London, Paris and Munich."

"That does sound suspicious," Shannon adds, "After the funeral tomorrow, do you want to meet at your house, Chloe, and clean up?"

"I appreciate all the help. Tennessee and Steve will need to be at the church at 9:30. So we will see you and Wayne then, too."

"There is something else here, Chloe. I can hear a tremble in your voice."

"Yes, Shannon, Chloe got another text tonight."

"Oh, another threat? What did it say?"

Montana repeats the text and tells her Steve doesn't think this phone is traceable. It's probably one of those throw-away kind, or a pay-as-you-go. They end their call and Montana and Chloe go back to the den to join the men.

After hanging up the phone, Shannon climbs in bed and snuggles down beneath the quilt and thinks, Chloe has had a lot of tough times recently, I'm so glad she's safe, and Tennessee, too. I'll go there when I get ready in the morning, that way I won't have to come back here after the service, I know she will want to go back to her house to clean up tomorrow afternoon, so I'll take some clothes to change into after the service.

Turning over, Shannon closes her eyes and waits for the embrace of sleep.

******

Tennessee rises from the chair and stands before the fire. Turning back to face Steve, he asks, "What do you make of all this?"

Steve looks up at Tennessee and says, "I think this is all tied together. Darrell told me that Preston and Charlie were staying at the Lamplighter Inn, and Ricardo Rossi, Marcus Magliano, Nathan Phillips and Bruce Johnson were staying at The Mockingbird Nest."

"What about Lorenzo DeLuca?" Tennessee asks.

"I haven't located him yet. According to Wayne, he should be here, too. So, tomorrow I plan on having a chat with him."

"Steve, I don't know. There has already been one murder, I am afraid there may be more. These people are dead serious."

Steve nods, begins to dial the phone and tells Tennessee, "Not if I can help it."

After the phone call with Shannon, Chloe and Montana return to the den and join the guys. Setting down the mugs of cocoa on the table, the girls look at Steve and sit down on the love seat.

Steve says into the phone, "This is Chief Blake, I need to check on some reservations." After a few minutes, he hangs up, and looks around the room and says, "Only Preston and Charlie are at the Lamplighter. They checked in on Monday. Ricardo, Bruce, Marcus and Nathan have reservations at the Mockingbird Nest. Neither place has a reservation for Lorenzo DeLuca." Steve dials Patrick's number and says, "Patrick, I've got info for you to check out. I'll give you these names and you can run a check on them. See if they were in the areas of the museums during the dates of the art thefts." Completing the call, Steve turns and says, "That's all I can do right now. I would suggest we all turn in soon. A lot of stuff happened today, and tomorrow, who knows what may happen."

"You're right, babe. I'll show Chloe to the guest room and make sure they have everything they'll need."

Montana says. "Uh, I'll be there in a minute, Chloe. I want to speak with Steve for a few minutes."

"Okay, goodnight."

"Goodnight, ladies."

"Steve, you talked to someone tonight about those phones. Did they have anything more to tell you?"

"Well, no, Tennessee. He's doing some leg work for me."

"Okay, I was just hoping to clear it up, you know?"

Nodding his head, Steve says, "I know, buddy. Let's turn in."

Tennessee says," You go ahead, Steve, I'll sit here and watch the fire die out, then I'll go to bed."

"Okay, see you in the morning. We will get this cleared up, Tennessee."

"I know."

******

Suddenly, Mary Smith is startled awake by the sound of a knife cutting the screen. Jumping out of the bed, she grabs her cell phone on her bedside table and runs out the front door. Heading for her car, she is unaware that someone is hiding, watching her as she dials 911 and as, it is picked up, she has just enough time to say, "Help me!", as she falls to the ground from a blow to the her head.

Officer Robin Lee is on call and receives the second 911 call from Mary's cell phone. Steve told her what had transpired earlier that evening and requested her to be alert for another call from that number. She quickly calls the ambulance and explains the situation, and then heads out to investigate. Coming upon Mary Smith lying in a quilt on the ground beside her car Robin checks for vitals, and is relieved to see Mary is still breathing, but she is unconscious.

The ambulance arrives right behind Robin, and as they lift Mary on the gurney, Robin hears a meow and discovers a patch-colored, short-haired cat, standing at the open back door of the house. Robin begins her investigation. Before she leaves, she dials the hospital and is informed that Mary Smith is going to be okay. Robin fills the food and water bowls and leaves Patches safe inside the house. She then returns to the police department to finish her shift.

******

Mary Smith awakens and realizes she is not in her own bed. Trying to sit up to get a better look at her surroundings, she manages to hold herself up, supporting her upper body by leaning on her left elbow. Her head is spinning and her eyes won't focus. There is a sliver of light coming from the door. Holding her head with her right hand, she eases back down in bed.

Trying to sit up again, her throbbing head is causing her stomach to roll and she realizes that any movement is making her very nauseous. Lying back and resting her head on the pillow, the room is still spinning. She tries to focus, first on the ceiling and, then, turning her head ever so slightly, she recognizes the curtain is pulled on one side of the bed.

She remembers, now, she is in the hospital. Oh...the can and the hiss..., she thinks, then can't remember. As her thoughts start to come back, she hears a shuffle on the tile floor. Looking toward the light of the door, someone blocks the light.

Someone is in the room, she thinks. Sitting up she asks, "Who's that, who are you?" Her eyes focus and she can tell someone is coming toward her.

"Who are you?" The shadow comes closer to the bed, she screams, "Help. Help me."

The figure is now standing beside the bed and she can tell it is a man. Leaning over her, his breath is warm on her face as he whispers, "You want to live? Then forget you ever saw me."

He pulls the pillow out from under her head. As her head falls back on the bed, she struggles to move away from him, but he's so strong. He places the pillow over her face and begins pushing it hard against her face. He is leaning over her and her arms are pinned down in the bed between his strong arms. She begins kicking with all her might.

At just the right moment, with what seemed like her last measure of strength, her legs kick hard and her feet meet his stomach. She grabs the call button, and screams, "Help. Help me."

The figure stumbles toward the door and, after catching his breath, runs from the room. Moments later, the overhead light comes on and the nurse enters, "Miss Smith, is everything okay? What's going on in here? Who was that?"

Mary sits up on the edge of the bed. She is breathing very hard, and shaking. The nurse comes over to her, and asks, "Who was that man? Did he hurt you?"

Mary shakes her head, then nods, yes, and tells her, "He tried...to kill me!"

Her whole body is trembling and she is still trying to catch her breath. The nurse comes around the bed and, lifting her legs, assists her in getting back in bed. As she adjusts the pillow beneath her head and straightens the sheet and blanket, she reaches for her wrist saying, "Just relax, everything is going to be okay."

After taking her pulse, the nurse reaches for the phone on the bedside table, she dials a number and waits for the connection, then says, "Officer Lee, this is Cindy Jacobs. I'm Mary Smith's nurse. Someone tried to smother her. Okay. She's in room 535." Hanging up the phone, she dials a three digit in house number. When the hospital security answers, "This is Nurse Jacobs on five. Please check the stairwells and parking lot for a man in a hurry, wearing blue scrubs. Thank you. "Then dialing three digits again, "Linda, this is Cindy, I'm in room 535, Mary Smith's room. Can you check her chart, and bring in a dosage of her pain med? I can't really leave her now. We had an intruder in her room and I don't want to leave her alone. I've called the police and notified security. Thank you." Looking over at Mary and seeing how helpless she looks, pats her hand and tells her, "Okay Mary, we'll get you more comfortable. I'm staying right here. Officer Lee is on her way and hospital security is searching for him."

Mary tries to thank her, but her lips are trembling, and all she can do is smile, weakly.

Officer Lee speeds through town, the sirens and lights of the cruiser are on, she turns them off and the noise stops abruptly as she pulls into the hospital parking lot. She puts the car in park and jumps out at the Emergency Room door. She spots the elevator and pushes the button for the fifth floor.

As the door opens, she sees the room number direction sign and turns to her right. She follows the sequence of the rooms to room 535. The door is partially closed. As she knocks and opens the door, she is met by Cindy Jacobs.

Robin smiles and says, "Hi, Cindy."

Cindy breathing a relieved sigh, says, "Thanks for coming, Robin."

Robin walks over to Mary's bed and asks, "Mary, how are you doing?"

Mary has stopped trembling, in the last few minutes, she has calmed her fear and now, with Robin's question, she realizes that she is mad. She looks up at Robin and tells her, "Officer Lee, I'm doing okay. You have to get this guy. He can't keep this up. He's going to kill me. I'm not going to say I didn't see him with Brent, when I did."

Robin has taken out her note pad and asks, "Mary, did you see his face? Who is it? Do you know?"

"No. It was dark in the room and all he said was, 'If you want to live, forget you ever saw me.' Robin, Officer Lee, it is not someone I know. If he knew me, he would know, I won't cower in a corner."

Cindy, standing on the other side of the bed interrupts, "Robin, the light was on in the hall and, as he ran past me, I saw that he was wearing blue scrubs and had dark hair. But the thing is, even though, he was moving very fast past me, I noticed he moved with a limp."

"That's not possible, Cindy. I saw him walk in the Artistic License Coffee House, Thursday night, and he doesn't limp."

"Okay. Did you hurt his leg, defending yourself?"

"No, he had my arms pinned down to the bed, but I managed to kick him in the stomach. When the pressure released from the pillow, I threw it off, and I could see in the shadows, he was bent over trying to catch his breath. He stood up and I found the call button, I'm afraid I didn't see him leave the room, but I'm sure I kicked him in the stomach."

"Cindy, do you think you could talk to a police sketch artist, so we can have a picture of him?"

"I'm afraid I only saw him for a few seconds, not long enough for a detailed description. But I did call hospital security to have them check the stairwells and the parking lot. I told them to look for a man wearing blue scrubs, and in a hurry."

"Good, I'll check with them before I leave. Mary, I'm placing an officer at your door. Cindy, do you know how long Mary will have to stay?"

"The admitting doc just wanted her to stay till morning for observation. He was concerned about a concussion. I'm sure she will be released this morning."

"Good. Mary, I get off duty at 7:00. I'll be back to take you home. Just rest, now. I'm going to get him. Don't worry you're safe."

"Thanks, Robin. I will. I'm really tired now."

"Thanks, Cindy. I'll go talk to hospital security on my way out."

"Thank you, Robin." Cindy reaches for the blood pressure cuff and takes Mary's vitals.

## Chapter Twelve

Wednesday morning, the skies are overcast at Castlekeep Ridge. Tennessee and Steve left after having coffee, and the two sisters are sitting at the knotty pine table in Montana's kitchen. Montana doesn't do a lot of cooking, but she can make a great breakfast casserole. As Chloe and Montana relax and enjoy their coffee, they hear a car pull in the drive.

Looking out the back window of the kitchen, Chloe smiles and tells Montana, "Well, Shannon is here."

Shannon comes to the door, and Montana calls to her, "Come on in, sis, the door is open."

Shannon smiles good morning and asks, "Any more of that casserole and coffee?"

"Sure. Help yourself. The casserole is delicious if I do say so myself." Montana laughs.

"What brings you here so early?" Chloe asks, pouring another cup of coffee.

Before she takes a seat, she hugs Chloe and says, "You! I wanted to see how you were doing after last night."

"Well, much better this morning. I slept good, even though it wasn't my own bed. Tennessee and I got up early enough to check out their Jacuzzi. That water sure felt great!"

Montana, taking another plate down from the kitchen cupboard and picking up a set of flatware, hands them to Shannon. "I'm glad you enjoyed it."

"Well, we did. I don't tell you two how grateful I am for you both."

"Which casserole is this one, Montana?"

"The ham and cheese one. There's buttermilk biscuits in the basket, too." Montana refills their mugs and sits down, her cell rings. "Hi, Montana here."

"Montana, this is Madison. Do you have a minute?"

"Sure, Madison. What's up?"

"How's your schedule look, today? I'd like to stop by your office and talk with you."

"Sure, you know about Brent's funeral this morning. I'm about to leave and go down to the office to check things out. I've been pretty busy the last couple of days. The funeral is at 10:00. So I'll have to be at the church by 9:30. How soon can you meet me?"

"I'll be there in half an hour, if that's okay?"

"I'll see you then." Montana hangs up her cell.

Chloe looks at her sister, "Is that Madison Blake, Steve's baby sister?"

"Yeah, she needs to see me. I'm meeting her at my office. I need to go to the office, before I go to the service. Shannon, can you take Chloe home to change, and I will see you two at the church. Okay? Don't hurry," she looks at Shannon, "enjoy that casserole and coffee."

"I will," Shannon says, taking a bite of the delicious, creamy, cheesy casserole.

"Will that be okay with you, Chloe? Going back this morning to get your stuff? Maybe you can take it over to Shannon's and dress there."

"I'll be fine, Montana. I am going to drink another cup of this delicious coffee and then I will be ready to face the world." She laughs gently. "Thanks again for last night. I was so glad I didn't have to stay at home."

"No problem." Montana smiles and gives her a hug. "See you guys later."

******

Before the funeral, Steve checks in at the police station and is met by Officer Robin Lee, she asks, "Got a minute Chief?"

After a sleepless night, Steve on his way to get a cup of coffee, stops and says, "Yeah, what cha' need?"

Robin follows Steve to the coffeemaker and tells him, "There was another attempt on Mary Smith, this time in her hospital room."

"And you didn't call me?" Steve finishes filling his cup and tells her, "Come in and tell me what happened."

After sitting in the chair in front of the Chief's desk, Robin takes out her notebook and says, "I'm sorry I didn't call you, but when you alerted me that there may be another emergency call from Mary Smith, I thought you wanted me to handle it."

"Robin, this case is keeping me awake nights. People close to me are involved. Hope Ranch was broken into and, Chloe and Shannon are being threatened. Just tell me what you got."

Flipping open her notebook Robin begins, "Cindy Jacobs, her nurse, called me at 2:30 this morning. I went to the hospital and interviewed both Cindy, who saw the perp run past her down the hall, and Mary. Mary said he came in her room and tried to smother her with her pillow. He told her, and I quote, 'If you want to live, then forget you ever saw me.' There was some discrepancy, though, Chief, in the description of the man. Cindy said that even though he was moving fast past her, she thought he had a limp. And, Mary said the man from Thursday did not walk with a limp and neither did her attacker. She said she managed to kick him in his gut, after she removed the pillow from her face, she saw him bent over trying to catch his breath. Then she said she didn't see him leave, as she was searching for the call button and calling for help. What do you make of all this?"

"Well, can Cindy talk to a sketch artist?"

"No, Chief, she said she only saw him for a split second, not long enough for a detailed description. Cindy notified hospital security and I spoke to the guard. He searched the stairwells and checked the parking lot and didn't find anyone. I've checked with Cindy and she told me Mary will be discharged this morning, I'm going by to take her home. Do you want to go with me?"

"Yeah, I do. This case gets stranger and stranger every day. You take your car and I'll drive, too."

******

Steve pulls into the parking lot of the Mockingbird Nest Bed and Breakfast. He enters the foyer as the grandfather clock chimes 7:00. Passing the dining room he notices guests are enjoying the breakfast buffet. White table cloths, fresh cut flowers, china and crystal adorn the tables set for four.

Approaching the registration desk, he is greeted by a friendly smile, “Hi, Chief, you're up and at it, and it's early. We've just opened. Can I get you some coffee or juice?"

"No thanks, Tommy. It's been a long night and I need to speak to Marcus Magliano. I need his room number and the room Ricardo Rossi is in, also."

"Well, let me see, Chief. They are both in room 24. In fact, they requested to share a room. They both checked in on Monday. They came in together, too."

"24? Can you point me in the right direction?"

"Sure, Chief, do you want me to call their room? They can come down and meet you."

"No, actually, I believe they're expecting me, no need to call the room. Just let me know how to get there."

"Okay, Chief. You go down the hall from the dining room. Their room will be at the end of the hallway, just before you reach the elevator."

"Thanks, Tommy."

Steve follows the hall and arrives at room 24. Knocking, he hears muffled voices behind the door. The door is opened by Ricardo, dressed in a tee shirt and boxers. Marcus is just coming out of the bathroom, wet curly hair, tight curls on his chest, and a white towel wrapped around his waist. He's drying his hair with a smaller towel.

He looks up in surprise and asks, “Hey, Steve. What do you want?"

Ricardo says, “I just rang room service for coffee. It will be right up."

"Where have you two been, from after the visitation last night to this morning?"

"Well, here, Chief." Marcus says, “What's going on, did something happen?"

Ricardo says. “That's right, we've both been here. Why?"

"No one else can verify your alibi?"

"Uh, no, Chief, just us."

"Well, I want to warn you both, if I discover either one of you have been up to no good, you will be prosecuted to the full extent of the law. I have prints from the break-in at Chloe's Moments Studio on Sunday morning and

I'm waiting on the prints to come back on the break-in at Hope's Ranch last night. I also have been notified of an attempt on the life of Mary Smith."

"Mary Smith?"

"Yes, she's the waitress that served Brent Mathews on Thursday night and she ID you, Marcus, from that night as well. Your prints are the ones that came back from the break-in on Sunday."

"I don't know no Mary Smith, Chief." Marcus says, returning to the bathroom. "It's hardly worth my taking you in for a B&E, as you didn't get what you came for, and I'm sure you'd bond out in no time. But I'm letting you two know, that if anything else happens to anyone or anything else related to this case, I promise you both, I'll be on you faster than bees on honey, so quick that your heads will spin."

At that moment, room service knocks on the door. Steve pushes past him and heads down the hall. Marcus returns from the bathroom and Ricardo takes the coffee tray and places it on the coffee table. They both stare at each other.

******

Pouring a cup of coffee, Steve goes to his desk and sits down. He opens the police file and studies, again, the witness statements, the report identifying the prints from the break-in at Chloe's Studio on Sunday morning, and Chloe's crime scene photos.

His phone rings, "Chief Blake."

"Steve, this is Patrick Reagan. I have the info you requested. All dates of the thefts are concurrent with travel dates." He adds, "I'll clue in the boys that are working the art thefts and get back with you."

Steve tells him, "Oh, by the way, the forensic report from Sunday morning at Chloe's Studio shows a match to Marcus Magliano."

"That's interesting," Patrick replies.

Steve answers, "Thanks for the info, bye for now."

"Bye," Patrick says as he hangs up the phone.

Just as Steve is ready to call the judge for a warrant on Marcus, his phone rings again, Steve answers, "Chief Blake."

"Chief, this is Henry Cummings, at Coast Car Rental Agency."

"Yeah, Henry, what can I do for you?"

"Well, Chief, I was going to call you to report a stolen car, but when I came in this morning it was parked on my lot. I had called to check if it had been returned. It hadn't, so I was going to come in this morning and call the family. I know things may get overlooked at times like this."

"Yes, Henry, but you said it was returned?"

"Uh, yeah. This morning with the keys in the ignition and a crumpled bumper with paint on it."

"He wasn't killed in an accident, Henry."

"I know, Chief. I've been following the Trevor Times coverage."

"The car was involved in an accident, a hit and run. Don't let anyone touch it. I'll send a forensic team over to see if they can lift any prints."

"Okay, Chief. Thanks."

"No, thank you, Henry. We've been looking for this car since the accident." Looking down at his watch, Steve calls the forensic team and sends them out to check out the rental car.

******

Montana lets herself in her office at the Black Widow Gun Shop. Walking over to the coffee pot, she starts the coffee. As she opens the blinds and looks out on the dreary day, she shakes her head, not a pretty day for a funeral. It's hard to believe that today Brent would be laid to rest, out in his family plot at Lighthouse Gardens. It is a pretty spot, the rolling green grass, the palm trees overlooking the loved ones resting there. Such peace...she sighs and returns to the coffeemaker.

Pouring a cup of the strong brew and sitting down at her desk, she waits for Madison to arrive. I wonder what she needs to talk to me about and why she didn't tell Steve. The Blake's are as close as my sisters and me. Her thoughts are interrupted by Madison coming in the door. A vision of gold, turquoise and sand, much like the beach she loved. She had a heart as deep as the ocean and laughter as light as its foam.

Smiling, she says, "Hi, Montana. Thanks so much for meeting with me. I know you have been busy with the relic robbery and Brent's death. But I overheard a conversation. I think you should know about."

"Okay, well, get yourself a cup of coffee and take a seat."

Madison smiles her thanks and pours a cup of the strong, dark brew, adding cream and sugar heavily, she stirs the coffee and sits down across from her best friend. "Tuesday night, I was working at the bar and three guys came in and ordered drinks. They were dressed real nice, dark suits and looked like businessmen. If you know what I mean?"

Getting up from her chair and pouring herself another cup of coffee, Montana says, "Did you recognize any of them?" Sitting down back at her desk, Montana waits for an answer.

"No. I don't think I did. They weren't well known to me, but then, I keep it pretty dark in there, so I couldn't say for sure. I may have seen them in town before."

Montana looks across at Madison says, "You say three well-dressed guys came in your place and bought drinks. Did they use a credit card or cash? Did they sit at the bar or go to a table?"

"The bar was full, so they took their drinks to a back table. They paid in cash. I happened to go back to the ladies room after they sat down. I overheard one of them telling the other two about Brent's criminal past. Could they have meant Brent Mathews?"

"Yes, Madison, I am sure they did. They could have been the three fraternity brothers that left the funeral home last night. The three guys went to college with Brent, Wayne and Darrell. They belonged to a fraternity at Florida State. Did they say anything else I should know, Madison?"

"Actually, as I left the ladies room, one of them said, 'We know what has to be done'."

Montana stands up and says, "Thanks, Madison. I'm glad you called me and you stopped by. I don't know where all this is going, but I know one thing, I'm going to find out."

"Good, I'll be going, then." She gets up, takes her cup over to the kitchen sink, and leaves the office, saying, "I'll see you later. Come by and let me know what you find out. I hope they were mistaken about our Brent Mathews. I've known him for years from the sailboat races. I never would have imagined him involved in something that awful."

"I'll let you know. See you later." Montana sits back down and calls Shannon. "Shannon, is Chloe there? Can I talk to her? I got some information I'd like to share, in fact, Put me on speaker."

"Okay, here she is. Did you see Madison already?" Chloe asks Montana.

"Sure did, in fact, she just left here. It seems when those guys left the visitation and went to have a drink in Brent's honor, she overheard a conversation."

"Really, tell us. Don't keep us waiting." Shannon jumps into the conversation.

"Well, she didn't hear all of it, but what she heard was something to investigate. One of them mentioned something about Brent's criminal past. I know he's been involved with the art world, and last night, Steve shared with us that those other guys have, also. I am going to check some things out before I meet you two. Okay?"

"You bet! We'll be waiting."

They disconnect. Montana, flipping through her Rolodex, finds a number and dials it.

"Patrick Reagan here."

"Patrick, this is Montana Castle. I need a favor."

Patrick leans back in his chair at his desk, smiles and says, "Sure, Montana, what do you need?"

Doodling on a piece of paper, she writes the name Brent Mathews. Asking Pat, "I need a criminal background check on Brent Mathews."

"Have you talked to Steve?"

"Not since he left for the station, this morning."

"Well, I told him that the travel dates of the couriers match the theft dates at the museums."

"Very interesting. I have talked to a witness from the bar that overheard a conversation on Tuesday night. She told me one of three men mentioned Brent's criminal past."

"I'll check it out and get back to you." As she hangs up, her cell rings, "Hi, Steve."

"Hi, Babe! The forensic report came back from Sunday. The prints match Marcus Magliano."

"Oh, really? That's very interesting. This morning, I had a visit from Madison."

"Did she have new information for us?"

"She overheard a conversation, 'about Brent's criminal past' and also, 'we know what has to be done'. I called Patrick to ask him to check Brent's record."

"Let me know what you find out and I'll do the same. See you at church."

"Bye, Babe."

******

Pulling into circle drive, Shannon follows it to the back drive of Hope Ranch. As they climb out of the car, Shannon asks Chloe, "What are you planning on wearing this morning?"

Smiling, Chloe says, "I'm hoping something will jump out of my closet at me."

Arching her eyebrows, Shannon says, "I hope you're joking?"

As the girls share a laugh, and walk toward the back door, Shannon says, "Hey, what's this?" Squatting down, she picks up the ballet slipper with her penlight.

Excitedly, Chloe exclaims, "*My other slipper*!"

The girls rush into the kitchen, Chloe gets a plastic bag, and Shannon drops the slipper into it with her penlight. Quickly, Chloe reaches for the phone and dials Montana.

"Montana, we found the other slipper."

"Great! I'll process it for prints. Bring it back to my office. I'll meet you here in a few minutes."

Chloe says, "I'll get my clothes, and we'll see you in a few minutes."

******

Steve is in his office at the Police Department. He is thinking about all the information he has put together on the Brent Mathew's case.

*Still, there are a few questions I need to resolve. But...I'm getting closer. I can feel it.*

As he is pondering this information, his cell rings, "Blake here."

"Chief, this is Monica LeBrec, down in the lab. I'm calling your cell because I didn't want someone in your office to pick up the line while we were talking."

"It's okay, Monica, what's up?"

"Chief, I went out to Coast Car Rental and lifted prints from the rental car as you requested."

"And?"

"Well, the car was almost totally clean of *any* prints. But I was able to lift two good prints."

"Did you run them? What kind of match did you get?"

"That's the thing, Chief, I couldn't believe the match. They match the ones we have on file for Sgt. Mike O'Rourke."

******

Shannon pulls her Beetle convertible into the parking lot beside the Black Widow Gun Shop. The two girls jump out of the car and run to the front entrance of the building.

Montana stands up from her chair at her desk, "Give me the bag and I'll see what I can come up with from this slipper."

Chloe hands it to her, "We didn't touch it. Shannon picked it up with a penlight and we dropped it into the bag."

Shannon and Chloe follow Montana to the back room.

Montana says, over her shoulder, "Great! After I check for prints, I can compare any I find through AFIC and, maybe, find a match."

The girls watch over Montana's shoulder as she works her magic. A few minutes later, she has found a clear thumb print, index print, and partial prints from the other three fingers of the right hand. Returning to the main office and the computer on her desk, Montana searches the data base, the Federal Automated Fingerprint Identification System, for the identity of the person who left those prints.

******

Steve just got off the phone with Judge Dorothy Neal. Montana calls him on his cell phone and when he picks up, she asks, "Steve, is there a chance you could come down to my office. Shannon and Chloe just left and

I want to share something, with you."

"Sure, Babe. I'm going to be picking up a couple of warrants this morning. I hope they'll be ready before the funeral. But I can come over."

"Thanks, Babe."

Within a few minutes, Steve arrives at Black Widow Investigation and Gun Shop. Pulling in next to Montana's Jeep Liberty, he climbs out and enters her office.

"Okay, Babe. What cha' got?"

"This, Steve," she shows a small video tape. "But, first, I want you to see these prints."

"I had the prints from the forensic team, Montana."

"Yes, but this came from the other ballet slipper Chloe found this morning when she went to pick up her clothes at home."

"Okay, let's see it." After viewing it, he says, "Well, I already have warned both Marcus and Ricardo that I was onto them. I don't want to make a scene at church, but I plan on keeping my eye on them until I can make my arrest."

"Now, this."

She places the video into her computer. Steve and Montana view the scene of Brent's murder in vivid detail.

After viewing the video, Steve asks, "Where did that come from?"

"This is from Shannon's surveillance camera, installed beneath her upstairs kitchen window, hidden in a replica of her Cape Cod home, a birdhouse."

"The short man is the only one who hasn't arrived yet: Lorenzo DeLuca. The son of an old friend from Interpol," Montana says, and Steve nods in agreement.

******

As the congregation comes into the church, the bells toll in the steeple. The worshippers pass by the closed casket at the back of Grace Community Church. The church is overflowing with people who have gathered for the funeral of one of their members. Doc and Mary Mathews, Brent's parents, are seated in the first pew. Sitting with them is Pastor Keith and Beth Stewart.

The organist plays 'Sleepers Wake' by the great composer Johann Sebastian Bach. The pallbearers, Wayne, Preston, Bruce, Charlie, Steve and Tennessee bring the casket to the front. As the pallbearers take their seats, Beth Stewart rises, and walks to the microphone, in the front.

She sings, 'How Great Thou Art' and 'Amazing Grace', and returns to her seat.

After a few moments, Pastor Keith rises goes to the podium, and begins the service with a prayer. His message is one of consolation and the reminder of God's promise. At the conclusion of his sermon, he asks Wayne Trevor to give the eulogy.

"Thank you, Pastor Keith. I was asked to present this eulogy by Doc and Miss Mary Mathews. Their son, Brent Mathews, and I have been friends since pre-school. We were neighbors, and our families enjoyed BBQ and picnics, celebrations of life. As boyhood friends, we played baseball, and together we joined the little league football team. Under the coaching of our dads, we learned sportsmanship. In junior high, we learned golf and in high school, we participated in wrestling.

"On summer days, we would take off on our bikes, and go swimming, and fishing. Our grandpas taught us fishing and our grandmas taught us culture with visits to the library, museum and the zoo, fond memories.

"As we grew into adults, we chose to attend the same college, and were roommates. We joined the same fraternity. In summary, friends, we were friends and teammates. Not a day would go by we weren't together. Today, we acknowledge our loss. But we smile at our memories." Touching the casket as he prepares to close, he adds, "My friend, I thank you for being there and for being a part of my life. I'm going to miss you. I know I'll see you again and together we'll share those memories, again."

Wayne returns to his seat and the service continues.

******

After the graveside service, the mourners return to their cars. Many would go back to the church for a lunch, and visiting with the family. Wayne and Shannon stop to speak to the Mathews and, then, walking back to their cars, Wayne says, "I'm going back to the church for a bit, but I'm going to join Steve and Tennessee for coffee at the Artistic License Coffee Shop to discuss all this. You're going over to Chloe's, right?"

"Yes, Wayne, the girls and I are heading over there. I'll see you later on, okay?" She hugs him, kisses him goodbye, and returns to her sisters.

"Are we ready?" Shannon asks them.

"Sure, but let's go for a walk first." Montana suggests.

"Fine with me." Shannon smiles at her younger sister and the two of them join Chloe.

Chloe tells them, "I just saw Preston, Ricardo, and Marcus leave. I think we need to follow and check out where they're heading. We know they have to go back for the relic."

"Yes, so, let's follow, girls!"

## Chapter Thirteen

The three sisters follow and detour from following the men. They follow another path through the palm trees to a cement bench and sit down. The three men look back and then proceed on their way.

The girls overhear one of them say, "I thought we were being followed. I see we're not, now."

Wandering into a group of cypress trees, the three men are unaware that the girls have resumed their following.

"Well, the plans are set. We are to fly to Miami this afternoon at 1:00 and meet him at hangar 57."

"We have a plane available, so we won't need to go through security."

"Ah, yes, everything is taken care of, that is great and expected, no?"

"Yes, for now. But this time we've run into some problems. The other art thefts were much easier."

"I know we should never have involved our former fraternity brother, Brent Mathews. He was not willing and, now, we had to resort to murder."

"No, not good!" Looking around once more, one says, "No, not good! But we need to be careful, now. I am sure we are being watched. We need to get the relic and disappear."

The girls watch as the three men walk away.

******

The girls look at each other, then Shannon says, "I'm so glad you both have your pilot's license, we need to be there, too. Let's go over to Chloe's house, park our vehicles, and change clothes. clothes. Then, we can decide who's plane we'll use and take a flight to Miami. Did you catch the time they're meeting him?"

"I believe it is 1:00." Montana tells them. Then, turning to Chloe she asks, "We're to be at your house, Chloe. But do you know if Tennessee is going to be home?"

Shaking her head, Chloe says, "One of the mares, Broadway, is about to foal. He's going to come home later and check on her. We might be able to get there and be gone before he gets there this afternoon. Isn't he meeting the guys at the coffee house?"

"Yes, Wayne told me they were meeting for coffee, to discuss all this." Shannon says, then adds, "We're wasting time. Precious time, girls. Let's go."

The girls return to their cars and head to Chloe's. Arriving at Chloe's, the girls quickly change their clothes and decide they'll ride to the airport in Steve's SUV. Chloe parks her vehicle in the garage and Shannon parks in the circle driveway.

"Tennessee won't notice, you don't have a car here, Montana. So we'll be able to get out of here before he discovers our plan. Who's plane do we want to take?"

Montana tells them as they climb into Steve's SUV, "We'll take mine and Steve's."

Chloe suggests, "I'll fly and you navigate, Montana. This is my element!"

Montana smiles at her older sister and says, "Sounds good to me!"

******

Chloe and Montana run through the check list. Shannon is seated behind Chloe. securing her seat-belt, she taps on the back of Chloe's seat, and says, "Chloe, we need to hurry, or they will be long gone by the time we arrive in Miami."

"Just a few more minutes, Shannon." Chloe starts the airplane, then speaking into her mic, "Request permission to taxi to a runway."

"Chloe, the run-up test is complete." Montana flips one more switch and adds, "We are good to go."

Chloe nods to Montana and speaks into her mic, "Requesting to be cleared for take-off."

Weather was perfect for flying. The sky was a brilliant blue, and the silver wings glinted as the plane soared, to a cruising height of 12,000 feet.

******

Wednesday, late morning, is not very busy at The Artistic License Coffee Shop. Steve and Wayne take seats at the table in the corner. Max serves them coffee as Tennessee arrives.

"I stopped at home to check on Broadway. She's still going to be awhile. The girls' cars are there. I didn't go in. I didn't want to disturb them." The other two smile and Steve's phone rings. "Steve here."

"Steve, this is Patrick Reagan, have you seen Montana today? I tried to call her office and her cell, but didn't get an answer."

"No, not since the funeral. The girls were going over to Chloe's to clean up from Tuesday night's break-in. Maybe she left it off, from the funeral, and hasn't turned it back on. What's up?"

"That's why I was trying to reach her, Brent's clear. No record. I don't think he knew what was going on, but he was killed because he found out."

"Yeah, that's what I thought, too."

"Did you find any prints?"

"Yeah, from the break-in at the studio, it was a match with Marcus Magliano and a print from the break-in at Hope ranch was a match to Ricardo Rossi. I'm still trying to piece together where Preston Reynolds fits in."

"Well, Steve, it's getting tight. Have you checked the places where they're staying?"

"I did after the service and they're still in their rooms. Have the warrants for Marcus Magliano and for Ricardo Rossi."

"Okay, I'll tell the FBI."

"I have another call, I better take this."

"See you later, man."

"Later." As Steve hangs up, he tells Wayne, "I'll explain everything, just give me a minute. Steve here." Ending his second call, Steve tells them. "I have positive matches on Ricardo Rossi from Tuesday's break-in at your ranch, Tennessee. I also have positive matches on Marcus Magliano from the break-in at the studio. I now have the warrants I need to pick them up. But, I also want to tell you some news, Wayne."

"Okay, shoot," Wayne says. "Brent is clear, no record. Montana had Patrick Reagan to run a criminal report on him. And I've arrested the man who ran Shannon off the road, Mike O'Rourke."

"Mike O'Rourke? But he's the one that answered the call and brought her home. I don't understand?" Steve, motioning for refills, tells Tennessee and Wayne the rest of the details. "Officer Mike O'Rourke met Preston and gang at the museum in New York City. He has been part of the plot for all five of the burglaries. He has checked into the security and has helped with the thefts. This time he messed up. It appears that your wife, Shannon, had installed a motion detector surveillance camera a few days ago. Unfortunately, I am sure she has watched it and shared it with her two sisters. Fortunately, we now know how Brent was killed and who did it."

"So, you're saying that Mike was there and knew about it, and that's why he went after Shannon?" Wayne asks, in shock.

"He didn't do the killing, Wayne. He was one of two men in the video." Then, turning to Tennessee he adds, "Thanks to your wife, Tennessee, we now have the identification of the other man." Steve's cell rings again, "Maybe this is Montana!"

******

The white clouds in the sky look like fluffy puffs of air. Ralph Andrews, the coroner, also works as a traffic controller at the local airport. Silently, he wonders if Chief Steve Blake is aware that his plane has just taken off for Miami International Airport. Smiling and shaking his head, he dials Steve's cell.

"Steve, I wanted to let you know that your plane just left here and is heading for the Miami International Airport. Chloe Hope is flying it, Montana Castle is navigating, and, oh, yes, Shannon Trevor is on the guest list."

"What?" Standing up, Steve asks, "My plane? Miami International Airport?"

"That's right, Chief. The funny thing is it appears those ladies are in hot pursuit of another airplane headed for Miami International Airport. That my friend, could mean trouble."

"Who's on the other plane, Ralph?" Steve asks, running his fingers through his hair and looking down at Wayne and Tennessee. "Preston Reynolds, Ricardo Rossi, and Marcus Magliano are on the first plane. Your ladies looked like they were on a mission, Chief. A serious mission." He chuckles softly, then adding, "I think you better check it out."

"Yeah, you're right, I do need to check this out. Thanks." Steve says. Sitting down, he tells Wayne and Tennessee, "Well, I have some news. Our ladies are heading for Miami International Airport. In my plane."

"Man, what are our ladies up to?" Tennessee asks.

"Trouble, I believe, Tennessee." Wayne chuckles. "We'd better get going, too. We'll use my plane, Steve. Mine's ready. I was planning on taking Shannon to Miami for a weekend getaway." Laughing and shaking his head, he adds, "I guess she's started without me. The sisters will be the death of us yet. Come on."

The three men quickly leave and Steve calls Ralph back to inform him of their departure.

******

The determined look on Chloe's face softens, relaxing behind the controls, she was in her element. She loved flying. The flight seemed to last only moments, realizing she was nearing her destination, Miami International Airport. Speaking into her mic, she announces her intentions to land. After receiving instructions, she enters the traffic pattern. Chloe eases the Piper Meridian to set down, taxiing on taxiway 159, to hangar 59. Chloe shuts off the engine, the girls disembark the plane and hide between two planes in the hanger, watching for the arrival of the fraternity brothers.

******

Preston, Ricardo, and Marcus exit the plane carrying the relic. Walking out of the shadows, escorted by several body guards, a small stature of a man; limps toward them. Lorenzo DeLuca smiles and after shaking hands with them, hands over the valise of money, and reaches for the relic from Preston.

Chloe recognizes her former admirer, and looks over at Shannon. They exchange a knowing look and a shiver, as they recognize the man, who had killed their friend, Brent Mathews. Unwrapping the relic, Lorenzo, lovingly caresses the jeweled cross. The stones glow on the relic as his short stubby fingers touch each of the rare stones.

Lorenzo's voice tremors with emotion as he tells them, "Another job, well done, boys."

At that moment, Montana, Shannon and Chloe come of the shadows.

Montana says, "Not so fast, gentlemen. I'll take that relic now. It should have been in my possession all this time. If the courier wasn't killed, he would have enjoyed life with his family and friends, instead of holding his funeral this morning." Pulling her 9 millimeter Glock, she motions to Lorenzo for the relic.

He laughs at her, nodding his head, one of his goons sneaks behind her sister, Chloe, and grabs her. "Not so fast, yourself, Lt. Castle. Now who's got the leverage?"

Montana looking at him and says, "Ah, Lorenzo DeLuca. Your father would be disappointed."

"Yes, you should be ashamed of yourself. Your mom and dad did so much for you," Chloe says to him.

"My mom passed away and left me a trust fund, my dear. With that trust fund, I sponsored these pieces of art. My father and I haven't spoken since her funeral. We never did get along. He always wanted so much from me."

"So much from you, what do you mean?" Chloe asks.

"He never liked my choices of companions, for one thing." As he motions to the group of men surrounding them.

"How were you able to get the pieces from the art museums? Shannon asks.

"Through us, Shannon." Preston tells her. Then he adds, "Marcus and Ricardo and myself have been involved in all five of these art thefts. Brent didn't want to be a part of it, so well, we had to get rid of him."

"Who killed him?" Shannon asks him.

Preston nods to Lorenzo, and he says, "I did. He didn't want to be a part of our group, so I extinguished his light," he chuckles.

Shannon comes forward and asks, "What about me, running me off the road?"

"That, my dear, was our friend, Michael O'Rourke. He also discovered your camera and I told him to get the video. Of course, he never succeeded at that, either."

"So you're saying that he was involved in removing those photos from the police station?" Shannon asks.

"Yes, again he failed there, also. He assigned these two to do the break-ins." He gestures to Ricardo and Marcus.

Montana jumps in, "I believe there are warrants on you two, Ricardo and Marcus. You won't get very far, even if you succeed in leaving here."

"Which brings us back to the situation we have here now."

As one of Lorenzo men reaches for Chloe, she asks, "Who threatened me via my cell phone?"

"That, again, would be me, my dear." Lorenzo tells her, then adds, "Now, enough chatter, you ladies are on your way to a one-way trip to the middle of the Atlantic." Laughing, he adds, "As my guests."

Moving toward Montana and reaching for her gun, Lorenzo tells her, "But, first, you must give me your gun."

Lorenzo nods at Ricardo and says to Montana, "You are outnumbered anyway."

Montana looks toward Shannon, just as Ricardo points his gun, and aims it at Shannon's temple. Montana swings her fist into Lorenzo's face, smashing his nose; he staggers back, and collapses on the floor. Turning, she hits Preston, her fist crushing into his gut. Preston bends over, coughing, trying to catch his breath, she uses the 9 millimeter Glock, and, hitting his head, knocks him out, falling forward, he lies crumpled on the floor.

At that moment, Shannon steps into Ricardo, first, stomping the heel of her shoe onto his foot, grinding into the soft leather loafers he is wearing. Elbowing him in the chin, he falls back, his gun falls to the floor, he loses his balance, and collapses to the pavement. She picks up his revolver, and turns toward Chloe.

Chloe, seeing the action her sisters have taken, realizes the goon has pulled his gun and is pointing it at her head. His arm is tightening around her neck. He begins to drag her backward. Choosing the right moment as he is stepping back, she pushes forward with every ounce of determination she has. His arm loosens, she turns around, digging her fingernails into his eyes, slamming her right knee into his manhood. He screams and collapses to the floor, not knowing which injured part of his anatomy to protect further attacks. The sisters turn, looking for Marcus. At that moment, the light comes on in the hanger.

Marcus is running to the door, and is confronted by Chief Steve Blake, who is pulling his gun and saying, "Stop right there."

The group is quickly surrounded by Patrick Reagan and his unit from the FBI, they capture and arrest Lorenzo DeLuca, Marcus Magliano, Ricardo Rossi, and Preston Reynolds, and Lorenzo's guards.

As they load them in squad cars, Steve says, "Oh, your partner, Michael O'Rourke has already been arrested, too."

# Chapter Fourteen

The Shetland Art Museum is spotlighted with bright lights, making the evening as bright as day. Guests are arriving for the evening, attired in glamour and jewels. The gaiety of voices reach the ears of David and Emilee Thomas, and a string quartet plays sonatas from the masters.

David announces, "Ladies and Gentlemen, it is my great honor, as curator of Shetland Art Museum, to welcome you. We have had a display of four relics. Now we have five more. We have on display, this evening, nine artifacts, five previously stolen from five different museums located in Munich, Germany; London, England; Paris, France; New York City, New York and Rome, Italy."

The guests form a line and follow David through the circular room of nine displayed items. Four had been on display from the previous show. The nine items are encased in glass atop black marble pillars. The oblique lighting on each artifact accents the intricate details of the relic, in amazing clarity. Upon completion of the tour, the citizens of Whispering Key enjoy champagne and hors d'oeuvres, and share a pleasant evening.

******

Montana Castle, Chloe Hope, Emilee Thomas, Trish Andrews, Madison Blake, and Beth Stewart are meeting for their monthly book club meeting, Chicks Against Crime, on Tuesday evening in Shannon Trevor's home. After serving themselves coffee and cookies, they relax in the sitting room, to chat about the past week and the coming trip to St. Augustine.

At Shannon's nod, Emilee stands, and makes an announcement. "Girls I have a special announcement. I am so excited! I want to share with each of my best friends that I am now opening a business. It will be called Candlewick Collectible Shop. I am inviting all of you to the grand opening next Saturday at 1:00 p.m."

The girls smile, congratulate Emilee, and begin their discussion of the current mystery book they are reading.

THE END

# Recipes From Murder at Whispering Key

# CHOCOLATE CHIP SCONES

2 cups flour
3 tablespoons sugar
1 tablespoon baking powder
½ teaspoon salt
1/3 cup (6 tablespoons) butter, softened
2 large eggs
2/3 cup heavy cream
Grated orange or lemon zest
1 ¼ cup semisweet chocolate chips

Preheat oven to 370 degrees

Sift together flour, sugar, baking powder and salt. Add butter, beat at low speed with mixer until blended. Not too long. Flatten mixture onto floured cloth or board. Cut into squares then triangles. Place on cookie sheets. Brush top with cream and sprinkle sugar on top.

Bake at 370 degrees 14-15 minutes Serves 24 scones

By Rebecca Harber

# MINI CINNAMON ROLLS

1 loaf frozen bread dough
1 cup sugar
2 tsp cinnamon
1/2 c butter - melted

Thaw dough in refrigerator overnight
Cut dough into 4 pieces
Roll each section to 1/8" thick
Brush dough with butter
Mix cinnamon and sugar and sprinkle over dough
Roll dough into a long tube and slice into 1" slices
Place slices on baking sheet and brush with remaining butter
Sprinkle with remaining cinnamon and sugar
Bake at 350 degrees for 20 minutes

By Lauri Ludy

These are yummy without glaze, just in case...

## CREAM CHEESE GLAZE

2 cups confection's sugar
1 3 oz. package cream cheese, softened
1 tbsp. milk
1 tsp, vanilla extract

Combine all ingredients in mixing bowl...beat at medium speed for 3 minutes...or until is spreading consistency....ENJOY!

# DEEP RICH CHOCOLATE BROWNIES

2 cups sugar
4 sq. unsweetened chocolate
1 cup margarine
1 cup flour
2 tsp. vanilla extract
1 cup chopped nuts

Beat sugar with eggs. Melt chocolate with margarine in saucepan. Beat into egg mixture. Mix in flour and vanilla. Stir in nuts. Spread in greased 9x13 inch baking pan. Bake at 350 degrees for 25 to 35 minutes.

Spread hot frosting over cooled brownies. Let stand until firm. Cut into bars.
Smooth Chocolate Frosting follows…

# SMOOTH CHOCOLATE FROSTING

1 sq.  unsweetened chocolate
2 tbsp.  margarine
1 1/2 cup confectioners' sugar
1 tsp.  vanilla extract

Melt chocolate and margarine in saucepan remove from heat.  Add remaining ingredients and 2 tablespoons hot water, beating well.

# TURKEY ENCHILADAS

1 1/2 to 2 lbs. Ground turkey or beef
2 cans of Rotel Tomatoes and Chilies per pound of meat
Add Salt and Pepper
Add All-Purpose Season Salt

Brown turkey, add salt, pepper and All-Purpose Season Salt. Break meat into small pieces.

After browning and meat juice is drained, add 1 can Rotel Tomatoes and Chilies, cook until liquid is absorbed.

Pour vegetable oil in a pan, make sure it is deep enough for tortilla (suggestions: red for beef, white for chicken, or cheese or white cheese, Monterey Jack cheese).

Drop tortilla into hot oil, allow to cook for 15-19 minutes. Place on paper plate to absorb grease.
Use Comet Rice for Enchiladas, add boullion cubes to rice for flavor. Bring to a boil add 1 can of Rotel Tomatoes and Chilies, heat to boiling. Do not stir, must not make watery or mushy.

Mix Ranch Style beans with Jalepenos (suggestion: Wolf's Brand Chili Beans).

Layer enchiladas, meat mixture. chili and cheese.

Bake at 350 degrees for 10-15 minutes, until cheese is melted and enchilada is crispy.

By Melissa Ann Carabajal

# LOBSTER BISQUE

2 Lobster shells
6 cups water
3 tbsp. butter
1 stalk celery (chopped)
1 whole carrot (scraped and chopped)
1 whole leek (cleaned, trimmed, and sliced)
1 medium onion (chopped)
2 tbsp. flour
1 1/4 cup heavy cream
dash of salt
dash of cayenne

Crack or grind lobster shells. Cover shells with water and cook over medium heat for 25 minutes. Strain. Yields 4 1/2 cup broth.

In a heavy saucepan, melt butter and sauté vegetables gently, stirring for around 5 minutes.

Puree in blender. Return to heat. Add cream. Season to taste with salt and cayenne. Add lobster meat. Heat through. Garnish with paprika.

# KEY LIME PIE

1 can Sweetened Condensed Milk
4 egg yolks
1/2 cup Lime Juice
1 egg White

3 egg Whites-Meringue
¼ teaspoon cream of tartar
½ cup sugar
¾ teaspoon vanilla

Beat one egg white stiffly. Fold into milk, egg yolk and lime juice mixture. Pour into 9" baked pie shell. Cover with meringue made as follows:

Beat 3 egg white and cream of tartar until foamy. Beat in sugar one tablespoon at a time, continue beating until stiff and glossy. Do not under beat. Beat in vanilla. Cover pie with meringue and bake until egg whites are golden brown at 350 degrees OR cover pie with sweetened whipped cream and refrigerate, may be frozen.

# PECAN - CRUSTED TILAPIA

1/2 cup finely chopped pecans
4 (6 oz.) tilapia filets
1 tsp. salt
1/2 tsp. garlic powder
1/4 tsp. pepper
3 tbsp. butter
lemon and parsley for garnish

Season fish with spices. Dredge in pecans.

Melt butter in a non-stick skillet over medium-high heat.

Cook fish about 3 to 4 minutes per side until golden and fish flakes with a fork.

By Lauri Ludy

# CRAB CAKES

1/3 onion - chopped fine
2 cloves garlic - minced
2 cans lump crabmeat
1 cup cooked shrimp - chopped into small pieces or use tiny shrimp
4 tbsp. mayo
1 tbsp. mustard
2 eggs - beaten
1 1/2 cup Italian style bread crumbs
lemon pepper panko bread crumbs

Sauté onion and garlic in butter until translucent.

Mix all ingredients except panko crumbs until well blended.

Form mixture by handfuls into patties of desired size.

Press into panko crumbs to coat.

Bake at 375 degrees until golden brown, about 25 minutes.

By Lauri Ludy

# BAKED BREAKFAST CASSEROLE

1 dozen eggs
1 can cream of mushroom soup
1 lb. breakfast sausage, bacon, or ham
2 cups shredded cheddar cheese, 1/2 cup reserved
1 lb. frozen chopped potatoes

Preheat oven to 350 degrees. Brown bacon or sausage, or chop ham.

Mix all ingredients in mixing bowl until well blended and pour into greased 9x13 pan. Sprinkle 1/2 cup cheese over top.

Bake 45 minutes or until fork inserted into middle comes out clean.

By Lauri Ludy

Read on for a preview of:

# THE SAILBOAT STRANGLER

## Second Book in the Whispering Key Mysteries

The Whispering Waves Harbor is surrounded in darkness, except for scattered lights along the dock. A cool mist envelops the harbor. The waves rock gently against sailboats and slaps against the shore.

Amy Harris scurries down to the sailboat, The Mermaid Angel, the catamaran owned by Chloe and Tennessee Hope. Looking over her shoulder behind her, she steps into the boat and whispers, "Hello, hello, is anyone here? Are you here?"

Looking around, she thinks, I was sure this is the place we were to meet. Sitting down she thinks, well, I don't like this, but...I'll wait a few more minutes, then I'm out of here...

She is startled as a figure climbs in the boat with her. Recognizing the figure, she starts to rise and, suddenly, a mist surrounds her face. She takes a startled, deep breath and collapses on the floor of the catamaran.

******

The flashing blue lights surround the victim lying on the beach. Yellow "Do not cross" tape marks off a perimeter surrounding the body. Curious onlookers encircle the scene. Dr. Ralph Andrews, coroner, is standing beside the medical examiner's vehicle that has arrived to take the body of the young woman, Amy Harris, to the coroner's Lab. Death by strangulation, it appears, but nothing is known for sure until the autopsy.

Dr. Ralph joins Patrick Reagan and Madison Blake, who are standing by a golden lab, Molly. Madison is owner of Madison's on the Dock, a bar down the beach, and happens to be a friend of Amy Harris. She identified the victim and was giving her statement to Patrick Reagan, acting Police Chief. Madison's slender, petite, form stands strong in the ocean breeze the waves swirling around her feet.

Her small hand is holding firmly to the leash attached to Molly's collar. "I'll take Molly back to my place, Patrick. She can keep company with my cream toy poodle, Peaches. My place will never be the same." She gently smiles into Patrick's twinkling blue eyes. "My Peaches will keep Molly so busy she won't miss you. When you're ready, you can pick her up."

"Thanks, Madison. I may be awhile."

As she walks away with Molly in tow, he smiles, thinking, That's one fine lady. He watches her golden blond hair blowing in the breeze and her turquoise jacket blowing around her...

Still smiling, he turns to join Dr. Ralph. The paramedics have placed, the body of, Amy Harris in a body bag, and as he watches, one of the forensic team slides the leopard print scarf, that had been found knotted around Amy's neck into an evidence bag. The filmy, silky scarf was thought to be the murder weapon.

******

Sitting in the Chief's office, Patrick reviews his notes, and the preliminary autopsy report he had just received. Standing, he walks over to the window and looks out onto the busy street outside. Friday was a busy day, it appears. Placing his hands on his slim hips, he watches the activity, he picks up his police cap and decides he needs a good cup of coffee, not this mud they call coffee, here. He leaves the police station and walks down the cobblestone street pass the court house, and walking the narrow side streets through the town's historical district arrives at the dock. The wooden boardwalk, leads to the bars and shops along the wharf.

Arriving at Madison's, he opens the door and enters the nautical atmosphere. Cypress wood had been used for the stools, tables, and the floor. A jukebox stands against a wall. A few patrons were eating, and discussing the upcoming sailboat races. Madison smiles as she sees him come through the doorway from the warm sunshine into this friendly, cool oasis.

"So, how's it going? Are you ready for Molly? Or in need of a good cup of coffee?"

Laughing, he tells her, as he sits down at the bar, "It's going, not yet, to Molly, but yes to coffee. I hear you make a fine cup of java."

"I sure do. I must have known you were stopping by, I just made a fresh pot" Madison pours a tall, brown mug, and places it in front of him, "Cream and sugar?"

"No, just straight and strong." As he sips the aromatic brew, the steam rises and he closes his eyes in pleasure, thinking, 'Now this is heaven.'

Ginger Reynolds comes in the bar and, seeing Patrick at the counter, joins him. "Well, well, Officer, or is it Sergeant?"

"Sergeant," laughing, he adds, "How are you, Ginger. It's been a long time."

"Yes, awhile. I heard about the discovery of Amy Harris on the beach this morning."

"Yes, did you know her?"

"Well, yes, I do. She was my guest."

"Oh, she's staying at your bed and breakfast?"

"Yes, she was. Have you notified her brother, Max?"

"Not yet. I'm on my way, though. I just completed the report."

"Can I get you anything, Ginger?" Madison asks, as she approaches the couple.

"No. Nothing right now. Actually, I was just leaving."

"As am I, Madison. I have to go see Amy's brother, Max. I'll see you later." He reaches into the pocket of his tight jeans and pulls out a couple of bills. "Thanks for the coffee."

Madison smiles and shakes her head, "No need to pay for that, it's on the house."

Together, Ginger and Patrick leave Ginger places her arm through his arm, turns, smiling, and looks back at Madison.

******

Max Harris is impatiently waiting for a call from Amy, to let him know where to pick her up this morning. His van is packed with trunks full of her new designs that the models will wear at the Fashion Show this weekend in

St. Augustine. He was so proud of Amy. She had graduated with honors, and was still able to get a fashion show planned. He and Amy were going to meet their sister, Jeni, at the hotel. It had been ages since the three of them were together...Patrick rings the bell and waits for the door to be opened. The sound of jazz floats through the open windows, the melody of horns and trumpets fill the morning air.

That's some great music, he thinks.

Max opens the door.

"Max Harris?" he asks.

"Uh, yeah, and you are?"

"Patrick Reagan, Sgt. Reagan. I'm with the Whispering Key PD. I need to speak with you, may I come in?"

"Sure. I don't have long, though, I'm waiting for a call from my sister, then I'm out of here." Max crosses the room and turns down the volume on the home entertainment system. "Can I get you something to drink?"

"No, thanks, Max, is Amy Harris your sister?"

"Yes, yes she is. Did she have an accident?"

"Well, no. I'm sorry to have to tell, but I discovered her body on the beach, this morning. I just received the preliminary autopsy report, she died of asphyxia. When did you last see her, Max?"

"Wow, dead? I don't believe it. Well, I saw her yesterday. She came to the coffee shop, yesterday, when I opened up. She asked me if I was able to get someone to cover for me, and I hadn't yet. She was in great spirits. She talked of introducing me to her boyfriend this weekend. And of course, she was excited about her show and her new fashion line. I called her around 4:00, yesterday afternoon, to let her know I had someone to work for me, so we planned on meeting this morning."

"Is the van out front the vehicle you were taking to St. Augustine?"

"Yes it is. I met her about 6:00 last night and we loaded it up. She told me she was upset, she and Chloe had a minor disagreement. I think it was about Ricky Lee, her boyfriend. Then she called last night to let me know everything was okay between them."

"Can I look inside the van, Max?"

"Sure, I have nothing to hide. Neither does Amy."

Picking up his keys, he leads the way to the van, parked below on the street. Max unlocks the rear door of the van and moves to unlock the side door. Patrick puts on a pair of gloves and begins searching through the containers holding all the beautiful designs. Patrick does not find any scarves in the whole collection.

Finishing, he removes his gloves and shakes Max hand, "I'm sorry for your loss. Are there any other family members you'd like me to notify?"

"No, I'll speak to our parents, and Jeni, our sister. I'll speak with her. She is probably in route to St. Augustine. When will you release her body? We'll need to make arrangements."

"I'll let you know. Okay?"

******

As Patrick is walking into his office, his cell phone rings. Reaching in his pocket, he answers, "Reagan here."

"Patrick, this is Madison. I wanted to let you know, I found Amy Harris' cell phone in the ladies room."

"The ladies room? Was she at the bar last night?"

"Yes, I spoke to her and her boyfriend, Ricky Lee, when I served them their lite beers. They seemed pretty into each other, you know. But then he left and she stayed and had another beer, then her cell beeped, she must have gotten a message, 'cause then she left."

www.ingramcontent.com/pod-product-compliance
Lightning Source LLC
LaVergne TN
LVHW050641100826
845148LV00011B/1938

* 9 7 8 0 6 1 5 8 6 5 4 3 0 *